Susan Wicks grew up in Kent, but has lived in France, Ireland and the US. She is the author of two previous novels, a short memoir, six collections of poetry and a book of stories. *Cold Spring in Winter,* her translation of the French poet Valerie Rouzeau, was shortlisted for Canada's international Griffin Prize and won the Scott-Moncrieff Prize for Literary Translation. Her most recent book, *House of Tongues,* was a Poetry Book Society Recommendation. She is married with two adult daughters.

A PLACE
TO STOP
Susan Wicks

SALT

LONDON

PUBLISHED BY SALT PUBLISHING
Acre House, 11–15 William Road, London NW1 3ER United Kingdom

© Susan Wicks, 2012

The right of Susan Wicks to be identified as the author of this
work has been asserted by her in accordance with Section 77
of the Copyright, Designs and Patents Act 1988.

This book is in copyright. Subject to statutory exception and
to provisions of relevant collective licensing agreements, no
reproduction of any part may take place without the written
permission of Salt Publishing.

Salt Publishing 2012

Printed in the UK by the MPG Books Group, Bodmin and King's Lynn

Typeset in Joanna 11 / 14

This book is sold subject to the conditions that it shall not, by way of trade or
otherwise, be lent, re-sold, hired out, or otherwise circulated without the publisher's
prior consent in any form of binding or cover other than that in which it is
published and without a similar condition including this condition being imposed on
the subsequent purchaser.

ISBN 978 1 907773 07 5 paperback

1 3 5 7 9 8 6 4 2

for Mara

PROLOGUE

She's reading the note again. It's hard to unfold, as if it's been kept in the envelope too long. The words have been scrawled with a cheap biro and she can only just make them out, even though she's read them so often she can still see them with her eyes closed. Or an after-image, floating diagonally upwards towards a spot over to the right and above her, burnt on to her retina in white light. She blinks. She runs her fingers over his signature. *Jason*. His handwriting's terrible. And he hasn't even managed to say more than a few words. *Sorry, Al.* He's always called her Al, like he couldn't quite convince himself she was a real girl, with a real girl's name. *I didn't mean it to happen like that. I meant to tell you properly – honest.* No kisses. Just his stupid unreadable name and the same word over and over. *Sorry. Sorry.*

She's blitzing her room like she's never quite managed to before, throwing the old Gap combats and T-shirts into a huge pile in the middle of the carpet and bagging them all up in black plastic to stuff into the bins outside. Old shoes – the strappy silver platforms she bought for the sixth-form ball, the flowered canvas baseball shoes she wore on the beach with him in Ibiza. His old grey sweater that she's been wearing for at least two years now, fraying at the cuffs and

1

elbows. The lovely interlocking silver ring he emptied his wallet for that time in York.

She isn't going to cry. He's not worth it. She can do so much better. As she tips another load of crumpled denim and polyester into the mouth of a black bag she catches sight of herself in the wardrobe mirror. The whites of her eyes have gone pink at the corners. Strands of hair are clinging to her cheeks, darker with sweat, almost brown. She just needs to let it all go, drift off somewhere where she won't have to look. But in spite of herself she keeps seeing it, that night at Casa Mia – she can still feel the bass vibrating through the soles of her shoes, the flecks of light moving over people's hair, and then outside the toilets that clapped-out leather sofa and something on it, someone, like a heap of coats heaving, separating, and she sees it's Jason. He sits up, his hair all on end, and she can see the whites of the other girl's eyes gleaming... She crumples up the pathetic excuse for an apology in her hand.

Minutes later she's letting herself out and pulling the front door shut behind her. She doesn't bother to take a key. She keeps her head down – she might bump into someone she knows. She picks her way among the oily puddles until she finds herself at the far end of the station car-park. Then she slips between the rows of parked cars to the brambles, the half-hidden gap in the fence that's always been there, ever since they were little. She used to play here on summer evenings, with George and Tim and Samantha, all the old gang, and they'd dare one another to worm through.

Further down the platform people are waiting for the train from London. A man's talking into a mobile, his head turned away. Kids are jostling for space on one of the metal seats, the concrete under their feet messy with polystyrene. She can smell their chips and cigarette-smoke from here, and sense their laughter. The ground under her own feet seems to lurch sideways slightly. She feels sick. She doesn't want to sit with a gang of mates and have a laugh and eat junk food ever again. She moves right to the end of the platform, where there's only a chavvy, wasted-looking female with a toddler and a baby in a three-wheeled buggy. The woman crouches down in her cheap jeans and high heels and reaches in to put something in the baby's mouth. Revolting. She can see it in her mind's eye, slimy and steaming. So that's it, is it? This is where it's all been leading, to a draughty station platform where a sleazy-looking bitch is knotting herself up into contortions over her disgusting excuse for a child?

But what else is there? It's too late now. She's had her chance. When all her friends from school went on to university she could have gone with them. But she chose to move in with Jason and start work at the call-centre. No one's to blame for all this, no one except herself. She can still see the expression on her parents' faces – almost like they didn't believe what she was trying to tell them. Not that they'd said much. But even then she knew what they must be feeling. She swallows. In a few hours her mum'll be coming back to the house to find the dustbins in the back garden gaping open, spewing out clothes and black plastic. *Alex, darling* . . . She winces at the bafflement in their voices. She can still hear her dad's relief on the other end of the phone the day she told them she'd had it with Jason, she was coming home.

She walks forward right to the edge of the platform, across the yellow line. The metal rails gleam in a bed of blackened sleepers and chips of stone. A trapped crisp-packet shivers in the wind. She squints towards the horizon, where the rails meet. Fuck them all – the man talking into emptiness, the kids with their greasy mouths, the woman swivelling on her spike heels as her toddler writhes and arches its back to be set free. The A-levels and university open days, the wind-blown campuses with their echoing sports halls milling with people. Jason's tiny kitchen with the mould-speckled blind and the view over roofs. Her mum and dad, even . . . None of it makes any difference now.

If I lean really far out I'll be able to see the train coming before it comes, I'll see the spot on the horizon like a bird getting nearer. I'll hear the sound of the wheels before they clatter over the points. And then the driver sitting in his little window. I'll meet his eyes. I'll be a dot, a bird, a twig breaking, I'll hear the thunder even before I see the spark.

Further down the platform someone shouts something. The mother catches at the older child and yanks him back, away from the edge. And then before she can do anything it's on her in a rush of wind and noise and lit carriages. She glimpses the pink shades of the little lamps in the first-class compartments as they whip past. Her hair lifts with the whoosh of air as each carriage flicks away eastwards and settles again as the last one disappears into the tunnel. It's too late. She's lost her chance. Through a blur she sees the young woman pick up the dummy from where it's rolled across the platform and wipe it against her denim thigh. The man with the mobile phone bends and slips it into a pocket of his briefcase. A lad with a shaved head kicks at a polystyrene tray until it slides over the edge onto the rails. She shivers again. Her eyes are hurting now with the strain of looking into the distance. The Eurostar's miles away already. She imagines it like at the start of the local news on TV, the girls turning their heads and waving, the apple-blossom, the train streaking across flat fields towards those chalk cliffs and then out under the Channel on its way to France.

ALEX

She can feel the train slowing. Through the slit between her eyelashes she senses sun and shadow, different intensities of light. She opens her eyes wider and sees rows of vines flick past. On the side of a hill over towards her right something shimmers. For a moment she thinks it must be water. Then she realises it's only plastic sheeting. Low corrugated buildings slide past. A line of new tractors; a level-crossing with drivers waiting in a queue of dusty cars, windows open and bare arms resting on lowered glass. Sheets blowing from a rope strung between two apple-trees. Then a row of bland-looking villas all raised on a kind of grassy platform, all with shutters in shades of grey or pale green, their scrubby gardens cluttered with swing-sets and tubs of french marigolds. A child waves from a swing and the train's shadow flicks over her, turning the fabric of her T-shirt a shade darker. So this is it. We're almost there. When she stands up her top's sticking to her back with sweat. The wheels catch for a moment and she staggers, the bleached landscape blurring at the corner of her eye. She stretches and reaches up for her luggage, easing the wet cotton away from her skin.

She hauls the rucksack down on to the platform after her

and stands for a moment, getting her bearings. A few passengers make their way past her on either side, towards the exit. A heavy woman in a dark dress is lumbering away, her string bags full of parcels. A boy jostles against her and trips against the rucksack, bending to rub his ankle and scowl back at her as he limps up the platform. She's on her own here. She follows them out on to the dusty forecourt and shields her eyes against the sun.

What does Susie MacLaren look like? Red-faced and slightly overweight, in a baggy T-shirt? She hasn't the faintest idea. But there's no one here who could possibly be English. No one here full stop. Only a couple of blue-overalled workmen under an umbrella at a café table, drinking something whitish in tall glasses. And a solitary taxi-driver with rolled-up shirt-sleeves, leaning against the door of his car to smoke.

He's looking at her. '*Anglaise?*'

'*Oui.*'

'*Vous allez chez Madame MacLaren?*'

At first she doesn't recognise the name, the way he pronounces it. Then she finds herself nodding, like the shy child she hasn't been for years.

She listens hard, trying to make sense of what he's saying. He's not looking at her directly, which makes it even harder. 'She asked me to come and meet you.'

She nods again. He takes a last drag from the cigarette and throws it away without bothering to stub it out. His brown arms are raising the lid of the boot, stowing her luggage, opening the car door and gesturing to her to get in. He slides in next to her. Finally he turns to look at her and stretches out his right hand. 'Damien.'

She feels the blood rising to her cheeks. Why do French

people want to shake hands with you all the time? It's so weird. In spite of herself she flinches slightly before holding out her own hand.

He's seen her gesture. 'How are your travel?' he says in English. He turns the key in the ignition and the car gives a cough, then starts to vibrate under her thighs. He draws out into the fan-cobbled forecourt, before turning his face in her direction again. 'Is this the first time you come in France?' She's suddenly acutely conscious of the sweat pricking in her armpits. The finger she runs along her cheekbone comes away wet.

The inside of the flat is so hot Alex is finding it hard to breathe. She feels a drop of sweat run down her spine like an insect and then dissolve, soaked up by the waistband of her jeans.

Susie MacLaren shifts the baby to her other shoulder and reaches to turn on the ceiling fan. The baby's red face is still scrunched up with sleep, little wet coils of hair sticking to the folds of flesh at the nape of its neck. It squirms and rubs its nose with its closed fist. 'The flat's been shut up for a couple of days, I'm sorry. I forgot to open the windows. It won't be this bad once you've had a chance to get a bit of air through.' When she talks the skin round her eyes squashes up into little accordion folds, hiding the white crows' feet. She looks as if she hasn't had a proper night's sleep for months. In the dim light from the small window it's hard to see where her body ends and the baby's begins. She pushes a wisp of damp hair from her face with the back of her wrist. 'There's a fan in the bedroom too if you need it. And wait a minute.' Without warning she passes the baby into Alex's arms, a warm, damp weight smelling of food and baby products and someone else's skin. 'Here we are. This is what you cook on.' Susie's crouching on the floor to rummage in a cupboard, her bare knees gleaming. She puts something down on the worktop. A grubby flex comes out of the back of it, ending at a three-pin English plug. The baby's fussing and Alex struggles to hold its little arms close to its sides, frightened of losing her balance. 'That's if you like cooking. Since I had Jade I don't really bother.' Susie straightens up and rubs the palms of her hands against the sides of her shorts before stretching out her arms.

Alex smiles politely, waiting for her to leave. She listens to the footsteps getting fainter down the stairs, the door to her own flat squeaking, Susie MacLaren's door opening and closing. Then she unpacks her things slowly and goes downstairs to the bathroom. She pulls down her sweat-soaked jeans and lets them fall to the floor. A moment later she's lifting her face to a stream of nearly cold water and closing her eyes.

She pours herself an inch of whisky from the half-bottle she stashed at the bottom of her backpack, filling the glass with ice from the little fridge. She's undone every latch she could find and the faintest breeze stirs the leaves of the scorched cheese-plant in its pot under the skylight. Here at the open window the temperature's just bearable. A breath of cool air lifts the fine hair on her arms. If I could live like this in just my underwear all the time I might just about get used to it. The place is so tiny – only this one small room and the bedroom no bigger than a cupboard really and the shower and toilet squashed together in that cubicle under the stairs – but at least it's got its own entrance. It's even sort of got something. The white walls are okay. And there's nothing actually wrong with the furniture. And there'll be the pool – didn't that taxi driver say Susie MacLaren's husband builds swimming pools for a living? She leans out over the sill, into the deep shadow of the house. Must be round there behind the barn, just out of sight. As soon as it gets a bit darker she'll go out and have a look. A couple of weeks and this will all be familiar – this small hot room under the roof, the harassed, blond woman in olive green shorts, the baby with its scrunched-up face. It'll be a part of her life – as much a part of it as leaving school, or going to live in Jason's flat, or childhood holidays in Jersey, or Ibiza, or home. For a moment she sees herself still standing on a station platform as the lit carriages flash past.

At home her parents will be doing their usual evening thing. Her mum will be talking over her shoulder into nothing as her dad yanks at the knot of his tie. They'll be wondering where she's got to and whether she's arrived.

'You will phone us when you get there?' Her dad just stood there waiting for her to answer or look up and she found herself nodding. Now the mobile's lying on the table at her elbow. She reaches over and picks it up, but there's no signal. Later. She'll go out later and investigate, when it's dark and there's no one to see her and wonder where she's come from and who she is and what she's trying to do.

Below her, somewhere in the village, a clock strikes nine. It's getting dusk. She can smell the neighbours' cooking smells, or is it a barbecue in a garden somewhere? She feels hungry suddenly and goes to the fridge. Susie's left her a plate of cold chicken and salad, under Clingfilm. She pulls the plastic off and starts to stuff the food into her mouth, licking the grease from her fingers. As she chews on a drumstick the clock strikes nine again. Can that be right? Nine o'clock nine o'clock? Is it the same clock sounding the hour twice, or two different clocks slightly out of sync? It sounded like the same one. Perhaps in an end-of-the-earth place like this everything has to happen more than once?

There's something rustling just outside. She turns off the light and goes over to the window, waiting for the darkness to give way. After a few seconds she can see where the noise is coming from. It's the woman from next door. There's a dumpy shape just on the far side of the hedge, moving up and down with a hose, training it first on one container and then the next. A smell of wet earth rises to her window, making her think suddenly of rain. *I'm dreaming this. I'm dreaming this whole village. Really I'm still with Jason. I'll blink and I'll be lying with my feet up on the arm of the old sofa in his flat with the TV on. Or I'm at home with Mum and Dad, I've never left. One of these mornings I'll wake up and find myself back on that station platform again.* She puts her plate and glass in a bowl and submerges them in cold water, then pulls on a T-shirt and a pair of cotton trousers she left draped over the back of a chair. Downstairs she lifts the back door gently so it doesn't creak on its hinges and picks her way across the gravel towards the corner of the barn. Above the uneven old roof the tops of trees are stirring. A cat slides past her, low to the ground, its eyes glinting. But beyond the barn there's nothing – only darkness and what must be the perfect place for a pool. But there's no smell of chlorine. No lapping water. No paving. Just grass between her toes and the low overhang of the roof with its cave of deeper darkness. Her eyes fill with tears and she blinks them away impatiently. *I'm just tired. It's been quite a day.* She steps back, away from where the edge would have been, if there'd been an edge. Something touches her face. *What the...?* But it's only laundry. She can just make out the shape of a woman's pale cotton sundress, pegged upside down so the shoulder-straps almost brush the ground.

She takes her mobile out of her pocket and walks out of the gate, towards the village, stopping under the post-office lamp to see if she can get a signal. But it's hopeless. She turns back uphill, towards a couple of cottages and what seems to be a barn in the process of conversion. She almost blunders into a pile of sand and a cement-mixer as she makes for higher ground. A dog in one of the lean-tos stands up and shakes its chain, giving a low growl. She tries the mobile again, but it's no good, this place must be off the grid or something. If I'd bothered to think about it I'd have guessed.

She walks back slowly. It's no big deal. She can write them a letter and post it tomorrow. That's what people used to do, before mobiles existed. Or there are always land lines, phone cards . . . Not sure I could talk to them anyway, without . . . Somehow she's found her way back to the village. Has she been walking round in a circle? Doesn't that sloping roof-ridge look a bit familiar, and the shape of that bush with the pink and blue flowers, like something crouching? And the car parked in the lane in front? She walks up to it and peers at its dusty paint. The light's almost gone now from the sky. It's hard to see properly. And yet she knows she's right. It's the taxi she came here in. She touches the bonnet. It's still slightly warm. *How are your travel?* She can hear the guy's voice saying it, his slightly mocking tone. As she stands there, the cooling metal makes a ticking noise and she snatches her hand away.

She's woken by cocks crowing. There seems to be a whole gang of them, scattered across the village. First one starts up and then another answers back and before she knows it

they're all at it, every fucking cock in the village, it's worse
than bells or traffic or sirens, she has to bury her head under
the pillows, it's obscene. And they've only just stopped when
the clock starts chiming. Seven o'clock seven. She raises herself
on her elbows and lifts a corner of the curtain. It's going to
be a hot day again. Already the shadows are sharp across the
gravel and the plants have that parched look. When she leans
from the window to see down into Susie MacLaren's garden,
the sky over the village has changed from yesterday's white
glare to a clear, luminous blue. There's a row of baby garments dangling from a line between two apple trees, their
little limbs heavy and dripping into the grass. Eight o'clock
eight. *Eight o'clock?* Christ! Susie MacLaren said she needed her
to be there, she had to go out at nine.

Alex runs her fingers through her hair and stumbles down
the steep stairs. Through the glass of the door to Susie's
kitchen she hears Jade whimper. When the door opens the
sound's suddenly twice as loud and she takes an involun-
tary step backwards. The noise seems to twist in her gut. I
must have got up too quickly. I'm not used to it. And Susie
MacLaren comes to meet her, in a sundress with big orange
flowers splashed across it like the contents of someone's
stomach. 'Hi.' She's grabbing up dirty crockery from the table
and plunging it into the washing-up bowl. 'Did you sleep
all right?' She stops moving suddenly, up to her elbows in
soapsuds. 'Are you okay?'

Alex tries to nod.

'Have you had breakfast? You haven't, have you.' Susie
dries her hands quickly and starts to rummage in a crumpled
plastic bag in one corner. 'Bread's a bit stale, I'm afraid. And
we're out of jam. But there's Marmite. And tea in the pot

still, if you don't mind UHT milk. Shall I put a bit more hot water in?'

Alex shakes her head. The baby's wailing louder, the screams accompanied by flailing limbs. She can feel the blood draining from her face. 'If I could just . . . do something?' She feels ridiculous. 'What would you like me to do first?'

Susie points to a basket at their feet. 'Can you hang those out?'

Alex nods. 'Of course I can.' But when she goes to pick the basket up it's almost too heavy to lift. She gasps. 'What's wrong with it?' The sheets and towels are saturated. A snake of water nudges its way across the uneven tiles.

'Oh, nothing. The spin's stopped working, that's all. He's supposed to come and fix it.' Susie bends and picks Jade up from the baby-seat and the crying subsides suddenly to a whimper.

'He?'

'My precious husband. Ex-husband, I should say.'

Alex braces herself and heaves the basket up on to her hip. Almost immediately a trickle of wet finds its way in through her clothes. 'He makes swimming-pools, the taxi-driver told me.'

'Yeah. He does.'

She says without thinking, 'Fabulous.'

Susie MacLaren's looking at her as if she's completely stupid. 'Yeah, it would be. Fabulous for the lazy cows he makes them for. Fabulous for their husbands with their fat redundancy cheques and nothing to spend them on. Great for when the children and grandchildren all come out from England for a couple of weeks to soak up a bit of sun.'

Alex feels her eyes fill with tears, as if she's been hit. She doesn't say anything. The water's running down her leg into her sandal, making a puddle next to her toe.

'You've seen what a wonderful pool he managed to build for us.'

'I . . .'

Susie shrugs. 'I used to think about it. But I've stopped. It's pointless. As long as he comes and fixes the machine he can do what he likes. He can build them all pools. Swim in them as much as he likes. Drown in them, for all I care.'

'I'm sorry,' Alex says. She moves towards the back door, her foot sliding in the wet sandal. She puts the basket down in the grass and starts to peg out the little garments one by one, twisting each into a rope quickly to get rid of the excess water. For a moment she sees Jason's hands as he rolls up his shirt-sleeves. Shit. The leaves of the old apple tree blur again. A wood-pigeon's calling from somewhere over to her left.

'Alexandra?' Susie's standing in the doorway with Jade balanced on her hip. 'Can you take her? I've got to go now.'

The baby squirms as it feels itself passed from one pair of arms to the other. It's starting to fuss and flail again, its face getting redder. In a minute it's going to let rip. With the warm, damp bundle clutched to her shoulder Alex follows Susie to the door, the sheet of written instructions crumpled in her hand. Tyres crunch on the gravel as the car backs in a wide curve. Then Susie accelerates and the noise of the engine rises, fading again quickly, muffled by the ivy of the stone archway. The baby's starting to cry in earnest now, arching its back, tears escaping from the tight slits of its eyes. She lowers it into the baby-seat and firmly but gently wrestles its little limbs into the straps. That's better. She has her hands free now, anyway. In a minute she'll go out into the garden again to peg out the rest of the clothes.

'You revolting child,' she says, under her breath. 'What's the matter with you? What have you got to complain about? You don't know anything about life, you haven't really even started to live yet. You've got all that to look forward to – school, men . . . You don't seem to have much of a father – I don't expect you ever really get to see any men at all.' Without realising what she's doing she's crouching in front of the child-seat, she's stroking the baby's soft head. 'You haven't got a clue about anything, you don't even know what . . .' The baby's stopped crying to listen. Alex dabs with a tissue at the small wet face and it twists up into a sneeze. 'That's better, snot-face.' She stands up to throw the tissue in the bin and the baby follows her with her eyes. 'Snotty-face, snotty-face . . .' she says again, teasing, almost singing the words. Jade pumps her short arms suddenly in Alex's direction and smiles.

The next morning is slightly better. And the next. She's getting used to the hot flat and the routine of child-care and housework. Even having to get up in the morning seems less of a wrench than it did. Sometimes she's actually half-awake before the church clock's started to strike seven. She doesn't need to lie there blearily and wait to count out the strokes again. And it isn't actually that difficult, looking after Jade. Once Susie's driven off to one of her clients she can relax and let herself be natural. And Jade seems to like her. When she comes into the room the baby's face breaks into a smile. When she leans to pick Jade up the baby reaches out to grab a handful of her hair.

And she's managed to find a place where she can get a signal on her mobile. It was the old guy in the post office who told her about it on Thursday morning, when she finally gave up and went in there to buy some stamps. She explained in gestures that she hadn't been able to get through and he showed her where to go, speaking slowly and clearly so she could follow what he was telling her. He even drew her a plan on the back of a used envelope and she saw that what he was drawing was the little triangle of grass on the edge of the village. She recognised the picnic table and row of swings, the public toilet, the shelter with the drinking fountain by the wall on one side. 'Ici, tout près des balançoires.' He pointed with the tip of his pencil. And that evening she finally managed to make contact. She's frowning now as she remembers the relief in her mother's voice. Stupid. Obviously I was alright. They'd soon have heard from me if something had gone wrong!

The little playground is almost always deserted. Just occasionally she's seen someone – a labourer eating bread and cheese or a young mother with a child on a little pink bike with trainer wheels. Once, a fit young guy with red hair, lying in the shade with his eyes shut, a book open on the grass beside him. Some fantasy, by the look of the cover – in English. She sits down on one of the swings and works it up as high as it'll go, pumping with her two feet together until the ropes are almost horizontal and the horizon rises and falls in front of her eyes like sea from the deck of a ship only faster. She shuts her eyes for a moment and feels the air whooshing past. When she opens them again the sky's clear, greenish, with just one bright star low down over the trees, or is it a planet? She lets the swing subside slowly, her heart beating in her ears. There's just enough light to see by. Okay, read it now. When her feet come to rest on the strip of beaten earth under the tyre seat she lets go of the ropes and feels in the pocket of her jeans.

She can just make out his writing, the slapdash capitals of the address crossed through and rewritten by her mum. She turns the envelope over, her hands shaking as she runs her finger under the flap. Inside there's another, smaller one addressed to herself at Jason's. Inside that there's a single folded sheet.

It's just a print-out, something from the local library – someone's asking her to return a DVD, that's all – something she didn't even know she still had. Or pay for a replacement. No note with it, nothing. Why did he bother? And not even worth forwarding. Stupid mother. What did you want to send me that for? She tears the whole thing into little pieces and stuffs it deep into the bin next to the remains of someone's salami baguette.

She walks back slowly, taking the long way round. When she passes the cottages the same dog gets up and trots towards her, its chain clinking behind it across the rough ground. She reaches through the scrollwork of the iron gate and it licks her hand. She scratches its head and when she walks on it follows her as far as it can, straining at its collar and whining, pawing the air with its front feet. Then it starts to bark. She hears someone shout something from inside the house.

She's come back to the low-roofed cottage with the hydrangeas. The wine-coloured Peugeot's still parked outside, looking almost black in the near-darkness. The driver guy's at home then. What was his name? Damien? Does he live here with a wife and children, or perhaps with a brother and his family, or alone? And how can he possibly survive on a taxi business in this tiny village? He must drive all over, ferrying people from the railway station in town to all kinds of godaw-ful places right out in the sticks. He probably takes people into the city, even – young women to the maternity hospital and old ones to buy new shoes. Meets Brits from the airport and brings them back here to their second homes.

She stops walking suddenly. Somewhere close by she can hear voices. And there's a cigarette burning. There's someone in the car – a man and a woman together, talking in low voices. No point in turning round – they've probably seen her already in the mirror. She crosses to the other side and makes an effort to walk past without altering her pace, looking straight ahead. It isn't until she's almost at the bend that she dares to turn round and look back the way she's come.

The car's still there, its windows in darkness. From here she can't even really see whether or not there's anyone inside. But the shape of the metal body itself seems to alter slightly as she watches – it's the driver's arm raising itself from where it's resting on the rolled-down window. On the other side of the windscreen the end of the cigarette glows briefly. Then the bulge at the side of the car appears again and in her mind's eye she sees a dark finger stretching to tap away the ash.

JULIEN

When he was young he hadn't realised sleep was anything special. It had been nothing then – no more worthy of consideration than the cassoulets they ate in winter or the pale green of the evening sky in summer – something you didn't even bother to think about. One minute your head was on the pillow and you could hear an owl hooting in the darkness somewhere outside. And the next the slats of the shutters were bright with sun. You lived your life like a healthy animal – sometimes you even dreamed you were a horse, lumbering along under your load of kids of all shapes and sizes – and sometimes the work was so hard you could almost have fallen asleep on your feet. By the time you'd finished correcting all their homework and preparing what each of them needed for the following day you could barely keep your eyes open. When you went to bed sometimes you even felt like an animal lying down in straw.

He didn't know what it was. He'd climb in between the covers and wait for a few minutes, and then he'd turn over into his habitual sleeping position, with his back to the wall and his face turned towards the door. And sleep would come slowly to meet him, shyly almost, bobbing and wavering at the corner of his eye like a solitary flame. And he'd feel himself step forward until his face was bathed in warmth and he was slipping, listing sideways in a slow exhalation of breath as the flame guttered, curling its tongue round his motionless body and drawing it sideways, out into the dark tide.

And then he'd start awake again as if a door had banged shut somewhere in the draughty passages of his uncared-for life. Bang. His knees would snap to attention, the soles of his feet prickling as if someone were testing them with an electric current. Under the sheet his toes would flex and straighten of their own accord. His body was a desert crossed by a colony of invisible ants. They'd keep on going until every last gram of flesh was eaten. Every shred of him had to be scoured away before they'd let his old bones lie in peace. Only then would the head of the marching column wheel round through 180 degrees and allow the whole company to file gradually away.

Tonight they were as busy as always. He felt them crawling on his skin and forced himself not to move or scratch. Random images from the past twenty-four hours flashed across his brain in the darkness, almost like dreams. But not dreams. The dusty shaft of sunlight from the high post-office window downstairs was as real as anything in his life. And that was M. le Président, surely, as the news crew had caught him that evening on TV, the wind tugging at his dark hair as he shouldered his way out from the belly of a plane. And here was the post-office again, that young English girl asking him for stamps. *Une timbre.* He'd corrected her, he couldn't help it. He'd wanted to bite his tongue afterwards – an occupational hazard, why did he have to do that? But he'd shown her where she could go to get a signal on her mobile phone and she'd seemed grateful. She was a nice kid, obviously. Reminded him a bit of Marie-Christine Fayard before she got married and had children – or was it Natalie? He'd lost track a bit. Sometimes in the line of receding faces there were one or two he had trouble putting a name to now.

After a while he turned on the lamp and fumbled on the bedside table for his glasses. It was all right. There weren't any ogres lurking in the corners. Only the odd cobweb Eliane never managed to get to, and his own bony feet sticking out at the end of the bed. He'd read for a bit – that touching novel Pierre had lent him about the Jewish boy and the marbles. And then a page or two of Montaigne. *The continuous labour of your life is to build the house of death.* Good old Michel. Trust him to have a wise word for everything – friendship, education, getting older, you name it – you'd read a couple of sentences and suddenly you'd begin to see your own life in perspective. You'd realise that nearly five hundred years ago all the really important dilemmas were the same.

In the morning he didn't feel as bad as he expected. He must have dozed off in the end, sometime just before dawn. And when the birds woke him he felt only a slight vagueness and a heaviness round the eyes, traces of tension in the muscles of his face and back. Nothing incapacitating. He'd open up the post office as usual and make a special effort to be cheerful and no one would notice anything at all.

Somewhere just out of sight Chéri was mewing for his breakfast. He took a half-eaten tin of cat-food from the refrig- erator and scraped congealed meat into a bowl. The little cat leaped on it hungrily, almost burying its head in the gravy. The church clock was just striking ten as he came down the stairs and unlocked the inside door. As he finished folding back the metal shutters it struck ten again. The shaft of sunlight fell through the window at its usual angle, swimming with dust. He turned on the computer and arranged his things on the shelf under the counter, within easy reach – the folder of stamps, the phone-cards in different denominations, held together by rubber bands, the Scotch tape and scissors, the sponge-pad in its battered tin. Then he went to unlock the door at the front.

The bright sunlight hit him in the eyes and he almost staggered. There was a queue already, Mme Alencin with her basket, Sylvie Daumier, and the red-faced Englishwoman from over at Les Vergers. He backed away quickly to the safety of the counter. You just had to take them one by one, be pleasant, make a bit of small talk. Just a couple of hours and then he could shut up shop again. This evening he'd drive into town maybe and have a pastis or two with Pierre at the Platanes. It was weeks now since he'd had a real conversation, about something that mattered. He'd take back the book, tell him how much he'd enjoyed it – if enjoy was the right word. Together they'd sort Sarkozy out, roll their eyes at Le Pen, wonder where yesterday's wiry, energetic kids had disappeared to. And they'd end up as they always did, remembering the war. Those moonless nights when you used to creep into the yard of Jean-Yves's shop and hide behind the stacked-up crates and bins, waiting to see who came. Some nights it would be one or other of the older kids, meeting some white-eyed stranger he didn't know from Adam. And off they'd go, the pair of them, the kid leading the way and the stranger following, south towards Lermitte, down the dirt tracks and wooded paths. How you'd be dying to cough or sneeze sometimes, or scratch an itch. And you'd have to stop yourself, your heart hammering. You'd have to squeeze yourself back into the shadows at the smallest unexpected sound.

He undressed slowly, smiling. It was good to take off his shirt and let it fall on the floor and feel the faint breeze from between the shutters across his shoulders. And the sheets he slid between were cool to the touch. He stretched his legs to the far corners of the bed and sighed, waiting for sleep to come for him out of the darkness like an open parachute floating slowly down, swaying slightly between the tops of the trees.

And crack. He snapped awake. The figure at the end of the ropes swung lifeless, its head drooping towards its chest. Only a dream. Or not even a dream, not yet. He turned on the bedside lamp and reached for the case of his glasses. The corners of the room came into focus, the cobwebs, the cracked ceiling, the voile curtains at the window, the dressing-table with its spotted mirror and his clothes laid out across the chair. He reached for the Montaigne again. *Life is a dream.* True. He could see his pupils' faces, years and years of them, stretching in single file to the horizon as if his imagination itself had brought them into being. He pictured them walking towards him, with their bright eyes and reddened hands and noses, up through the village until they came to the school and through the high gates into the yard with its shelter and scrubby plane tree. Martin Verge, Magali Verge, Antoine du Boucher, Alice Verge. Oui, Monsieur. All there, all present and correct. And no older, no more set in their ways or tired or disillusioned than they were then. *When we sleep we are awake, and when awake we sleep.*

He left the 2CV in the shade of a plane tree and let himself stand looking for a moment at the river. The Taux was sluggish at this point, a wide fan of water above the green-slimed lip of the weir, almost stationary under a skin of floating leaves. A young lad was sitting on the wall, half-turned to the water, by the chalked sign advertising bikes and canoes to rent – the son of old Maurisse, the owner of the Platanes café – still recognisable as the little kid who used to sneak out when his dad wasn't looking and ring the bicycle bells and scamper off again before anyone could work out who it was. But almost grown up now. Playing with some electronic device, even. Out of the corner of his eye Julien saw him move his forefinger, tapping in some sort of command. And out of the corner of his eye too he saw a girl coming forward, hesitating on the narrow pavement before she ran across – a dark, curly-haired girl he seemed to half recognise as one of his ex-pupils from a few years back. The boy put away the thing in his lap and stood up slowly. They kissed each other on both cheeks and stood there with their heads close together, apparently staring at the debris floating on the surface. They were waiting for him to leave, obviously. What did you expect? He turned his back on them and set his sights on the mouth of the little street that led back up towards the square. They were just children, that was all it was. They just wanted to be on their own. That was what it was like when you were about sixteen, remember? And now you weren't even their teacher, you couldn't tell them to sit still and put their hands on their heads while you considered how best to deal with the situation. All you were was an old man who just happened to be in their way.

'My God, you look miserable! Has someone just broken your last bottle of *hors d'âge*, or what? *Allez, mon vieux*, get your mouth round a slug of this.' Pierre was already there, squinting up at him from a pool of shade, pushing a glass towards him across the green metal table.

Julien sat down heavily and pulled the carafe towards him. He filled the glass almost to the rim with water, watching the clear liquid turn to milk. '*A la tienne.*' He raised it to his lips and felt the cool aniseed slip down.

For a while they sat in silence. In the square someone started a moped and rode away, the sound fading quickly, swallowed by old stone walls. From the river came the twitter of birds. Pierre was leaning back in his chair, studiously not meeting his eyes.

Julien reached into the old canvas bag he carried and brought out the book. He laid it face down on the table.

Pierre reached across and picked it up. 'What did you think?'

'Not bad.' He had a sudden sharp vision of the little boy in the story, the people who were kind to him against all odds, the magic that somehow kept him safe. He fought against an almost overwhelming longing to close his eyes.

He felt Pierre's hand on his sleeve. 'Are you all right?'

'Just haven't been sleeping too well. Be okay tonight.'

'Hmm.' Pierre rubbed his chin, his unfinished cigarette smoking in the ash-tray. Around them the air was blue. After a while he picked the butt up and squashed it against the glass base. 'How long's this been going on?'

He felt himself shrug. 'It never used to happen. Always slept like a log until now. Must just be something that gets you as you get older.'

The two young kids swung past them, hand in hand, and disappeared through the open doorway. From inside you could hear their voices, exclaiming and laughing, the father's deeper tones asking a question. Then the son, uninterrupted. It sounded as if he was explaining something. The girl laughed again.

Pierre reached out and patted him roughly on the shoulder. 'I know. It's a bastard.'

Julien shrugged. A fragment of Montaigne came into his mind with all the sharp clarity of a revelation, but he pushed it away. Trust old Michel to have been there already. 'And you?' he said.

But Pierre's answer was drowned out by the rising noise from inside the café – the voices louder now, and closer. They seemed to be starting some sort of argument. The two men fell silent, listening. It was Jeannine Maurisse's voice, as high and querulous as an old woman's. You'd have thought she was being half-strangled. A chair scraped on the tiled floor as the boy shouted something. And a moment later the young couple burst from the doorway, half-running, holding hands, making towards the river. Then Maurisse himself was standing there among the swaying plastic ribbons. He crossed his arms over his belly, shaking his head silently as he stared after them, as if expecting them still to be there. After a while he raised his eyes to watch the swallows flickering in and out of the eaves.

That night again he lay for hours staring into the darkness. He strained his ears to hear the slightest sound, but there was nothing. Not a single car passing in the distance, not a single footstep, not a single human voice. He turned over and the bed creaked companionably. Then the silence re-established itself, as impenetrable as before. His own heart thudded in his ears and he found himself attentive to any small syncopation, any tiny hiccup that might herald a sudden racing or – God forbid – a lurching to a stop.

And then at last he heard the cock at La Grange give a kind of croak. And again, in better voice, as light began to seep through the shutters. The church clock roused itself from its night's silence and struck six, six. A wood-pigeon cooed in the weeping willow that grew on the bank just outside his window, and finally sleep seemed to be coming nearer, like someone in the far distance walking towards him along a narrow path. It had the shape of a man, tall and wiry, with a weather-beaten face and old clothes that were stiff with dried sweat, a battered hat with a wide brim to protect him against rain and sun. A stick that punctured the ground with every step he took. It was like a kind of pain coming. As he drifted off he saw a momentary clear picture – the man was just starting out, hoisting his pack on to his thin shoulders, unfolding and refolding the map from its clear plastic sheath. If you put your ear to the ground, you could just feel the faint vibration of footsteps. Or was it your own heartbeat you were hearing? But the sound was miles away still, somewhere far to the north or east.

He woke to hear someone rattling the front door of the post office. A buzz of voices rose from the steps outside. He thought he could make out Eliane's, and something in a foreign language – was it English? He opened the shutters a fraction of a centimetre and put his eye to the crack. Yes – the little English girl, with that MacLaren woman's baby in a pushchair, and the red-haired boy from over towards Seyrac. That was quick work! He found himself whistling inwardly in admiration. But they were all the same, that was all they ever wanted. He pulled on his old blue trousers and a sweater and stumbled, blinking, down the narrow stairs, the big key in his hand.

'Yes? So. Who's first?' He heard himself almost bark the words. In front of him they went suddenly quiet, the boy's smile fading as if he'd been reprimanded, the girl looking down at her fingers on the buggy's handles. The baby started to cry.

Eliane stood there with her hands on her hips and met his eyes belligerently. 'Monsieur forgot to set his alarm-clock, perhaps.' She reached under the counter to slide the bolt open and squeezed herself and her bulging string bag through to the other side. She held out her hand for the key.

He passed his hand across his face with embarrassment. His skin felt rubbery, the surface as rough as sand-paper. He hadn't had time to shave. What must he look like? And the line stretched to the front door and beyond. 'Next?' he shouted. Were they laughing at him? The faces seemed to waver, shrinking back slightly towards the steps outside.

He served them, one after the other. Stamps, a phone-card, a parcel to Christiane du Boucher's old mother who was in the *asile* in Aubrillac. A fishing licence. And then Eliane was at his elbow with a bowl of steaming coffee and wedges of buttered bread. Red-currant jelly. Her own, probably, from the currant-bushes in that ramshackle garden of hers. He blinked as the steam made his eyes water. How did she do it? How did she manage to be so patient with him after all these years of getting almost nothing in return?

At last the small room was empty. He dipped a lump of bread into his *café au lait* and watched the little pearls of butter rise to the surface. Well, that was a near miss. You were lucky there. If you go on like that they won't want you; you'll lose this little job and what are you going to do with yourself then? No good pretending they'll look after you, because they won't. They'll think you've decided to hit the bottle, the way Marcel did. They'll say it runs in the family – that you can't ever escape it, it's in the blood. Or they'll think you're just going senile – multi-infarct, or Altzheimer's. And if you lose the job you'll have to find somewhere else to live. Well, at least he'd got his small savings; he hadn't really touched anything since Marcel died. He'd be able to find somewhere. But what if it was poverty of soul that was the real problem? What was it Michel said: *Poverty of goods is easily cured; poverty of soul, impossible?* What if the place where your life used to be starts to gape open, full of rotting holes? All that wisdom you used to pretend you were passing on, where's it all got to, why can't you tap into some of it on your own behalf? He felt something rub against him, as Chéri wound himself smoothly between his ankles, and he reached down and ran his hand through the dark fur.

Eliane had done her best. Never one to be very interested in cleaning, she'd nevertheless managed to make his bedroom seem slightly less forbidding. The cobwebs were still there in the corners, but the bed was freshly made up, the bottom sheet wrapped smoothly round the bolster, the top one stretching unwrinkled from the carved headboard to the foot. She'd even dusted the top of the dressing-table: his brush and comb were slightly displaced. Perhaps tonight would be different. Perhaps he'd suddenly find himself sinking into sleep as if into a snowdrift, he'd lie curled up in whiteness until the crystals on his eyelids started to glow red in the light from the rising sun.

And at first, yes, here it was, he was floating gently above himself on a field of snow or cloud, listing sideways and then sucked away into a dark wave that carried him far out where the islands were. Snow, stars, sea, a rocky cove – nothing between him and the world but this thin veil of sleep that made it all somehow more transparent than it ever was in his waking life. Marcel was still alive – his funny little brother passing all his exams with flying colours, what about that? – leaning forward to thump the table as they all doubled up in laughter at one of his crazy jokes. And Eliane was younger and slimmer in those days – almost pretty. She'd even brought him a bunch of wild flowers once – he still remembered it – a jam-jar on the window-sill crowded with cowslips and honeysuckle and wild roses. She'd worn her hair longer, pinned up behind in an enamel clasp. He searched his memory, trying to pinpoint the time when the gruff, slightly bullying tone she used with him now had begun.

But it felt as if his life had been like this always. Somewhere at bottom he'd always been a candidate for bullying. Eliane had always seemed fond of him, with her rough kindness and sharp words. Marcel had been marked out by death even from the beginning. The long lines of children had always stretched out behind him into a future of dead-end jobs or escape to the city, and he had always been giving them everything he could and tearing his hair that he couldn't give them more. And then he'd watched them turn into farmers and labourers, power-plant workers, mothers and fathers of families, shopkeepers, ghosts, until at last he'd begun to forget even their names.

Bernard Verge, with the tuft of hair that stood up on his crown, always only half-awake. Magali Verge, delightful, how she'd come to him as a little child and stood wordless at his knee. Olivier Simon, quick and laughing and intelligent, off to Toulouse before you could say knife. He could see them now, bent over their exercise books, or jostling one another as they waited under the plane-tree for the rackety little bus that would take them home to their outlying hamlets and farms. So many new ideas he must have implanted in their minds – and for what? *A man may live long, yet live very little.* He raised himself on one elbow and felt for the pillow, beating it into a better shape. He turned to face the wall and stared into its intense darkness, wrapping the length of his spine in the thin sheet, his back towards the door.

But it was no good. He couldn't manage to drop off. Whatever he did it seemed the magical state of oblivion would always elude him. He cursed under his breath and sat up, throwing the sheet off and swinging his feet to the floor-boards. The kids were all still there, just under his eyelids, rows and rows of them, several generations, going back as far as he could see.

The schoolhouse was in complete darkness. He let himself in with the key they'd never thought to ask him to give back, and climbed the narrow stairs to the schoolmaster's living quarters above. He flicked a switch on the wall, but nothing happened. They must have turned the power off at the mains. He opened a pair of shutters and the moon swam out above the trees, shining into the room's corners and showing up the darker place under the window where his narrow bed used to stand. He ran his hand along the window-sill and smiled, still thinking of Eliane's jam-jars. Perhaps he hadn't lived as little as he might have done.

He went downstairs. The schoolroom still had almost all its furniture, all the old tables and chairs he'd sat looking at hour after hour for years. He could almost see Catherine Morand, sulky over by the window, hugging the top of the old radiator and looking up at him sideways, her head resting on her arm. And one of the Verge kids – Bernard, was it? – at the desk just in front of his own, kicking the leg with the toe of his boot. *That's enough, Bernard.* He could hear his own voice saying it testily, as if they were all still there with him. *What have you got to say to that, Catherine? That's better. Is there something you need help with? Yes, what is it? What's the matter with you all this morning? Are you all still half asleep, or what?*

From their seats the children stared at him silently. The little ones looked up from their drawing and rubbed their faces and sneezed. A couple of ten-year-old girls were giggling. One cupped her hand and whispered something in the other's ear. In the far corner one of the big boys lounged on two chair-legs, his back against the wall. *What is this?* He can feel the strain in his own voice. *What's the matter with you? Why aren't you working? Get your book out and open it at page 211,* he shouts to the boy at the back. *And what's that in your mouth, Bernard, are you chewing something? You can take it out this minute, do you hear me? Come up here, that's right, and let me see you put it in the bin.*

They're ignoring him. The big boy's standing up, looking him straight in the eye as he climbs on to his seat and raises his arms as if to conduct an orchestra. The girls cling to each other, waiting for his anger to explode. Even the little ones are goggling now, their wax crayons suspended over the big sheets of kitchen paper. Something starts to drip down, making a dark puddle under Magali Verge's chair.

And he's speaking to them, trying to stay calm, not raising his voice, reasoning with them, appealing to their better natures – but in the end he can't help it, he's beside himself with some kind of intense emotion – grief or anger, he can't tell which it is – beating his fist on the teacher's table in front of him, the tears running down his cheeks and splashing the dark scarred wood.

And then at last they do seem to listen. One by one the hoots and jeers and laughter die in the children's throats. He's exhausted. He sits down on the teacher's chair and rests his head on the desk in front of him. Gradually he lets his eyes close. And Martin Verge, Olivier Simon, Bernard Verge, Susanne Arnot, Christiane Boisselet, Catherine Morand, Natalie Fayard, Magali Verge, Antoine du Boucher all stand up silently and file out past his heavy head towards the open schoolroom door.

PETE

He had succeeded in creating a paradise on earth. He lay back and squinted up at the umbrella with its dark wood spokes, like a perfect green wheel. The sun was just visible through the fabric, the sky pulsing heat. He stretched out his legs and felt its glow along the whole length of them, from mid-thigh down over his knees and shins and the brown arches of his feet to the inside edge of his big toes, a mild, pleasurable burn.

In a minute it would get too much and he'd take a quick dip to cool off. If he raised his head just slightly he could catch the glitter of light on the ripples, the faintest whiff of chlorine from the surface at the deep end. If he sat up completely he'd see his whole domain spread out in front of him, the neat paving to the pool's edges, the crescent of submerged shallow steps at the far end, and on the bottom that stunning mosaic with its pattern of leaping dolphins in different shades of blue. If, when he was younger, someone had told him this was where it was all leading, he wouldn't have believed them. The perfect place to stop. He'd have laughed in their faces, assuming they were trying to make him look a complete fool.

And now here he was. Here he and Lizzie were – and Jack, in his holidays from university. From over on the grass to his right Jack's voice came to him faintly – talking to that English girl he seemed to have picked up somewhere a couple of days ago. He could just make out the rhythm of question and answer, the higher voice of the girl. The clip clop of the ping-pong ball bouncing backwards and forwards. Then laughter and a short silence as they delved with their bats in the wiry grass, somewhere not too far from where he lay.

He heard footsteps on the paving-stones, and the lounger next to his scraped across the ground as someone put their weight on it. He lifted his head, shielding his eyes with his hand.

But it was Liz, with a sarong over her swimsuit and four plastic beakers of something on a tray. 'Lemon barley.' She called the kids over. 'Wish I had something to give you all to go with it – biscuits or cake or something. Remember that gorgeous date and walnut we used to get at Sainsbury's?'

'You should have told me,' Jack said. 'I could have brought you some.'

'Oh . . .' She waved his suggestion away. 'Are you two kids getting on alright?'

The girl looked embarrassed. Jack grinned at her and said easily, 'We're fine, Mum. Don't worry about us. If we want something we'll just help ourselves, okay?'

'Right.' She looked faintly put out. Somewhere over to the front of the house a car door slammed. One of the summer tenants. Going out sightseeing, no doubt, or to a local cellar to taste the wine. Rather them than him. He smelled the petrol fumes from the road as their car accelerated away.

Liz stood up, brushing an insect from her skirt. She reached over to pick up the tray and he could see the reddish, freckled skin between her breasts, a little fan of fine wrinkles spreading upwards towards the base of her neck . He said, 'Are you going inside already? You've only just come out.'

'I've got things to do.'

'Like what?'

'I'm in the middle of an email to Jo. They've just come back from Winchester. And we're going to tennis at four, remember?'

'Shit,' he said.

She looked round to see where the kids were, but they'd already gulped down their drinks and gone. He heard the double rap of the ball as someone served. He got to his feet and altered the position of his sun-bed slightly, so his head and most of his body would still be in shade. From somewhere above him she said, 'I'm going in, then. Another half an hour or so and then we should think about leaving.'

He didn't answer. As he lay back down he could still see the brightness even through his closed eyelids. Her sandals flapped away, towards the far end of the pool and the dark kitchen beyond.

The water was delicious. As he surfaced the world seemed to fall away from his face in flakes of light. He trod water and under him the ceramic dolphins rippled and swayed. Beyond the deep end a line of old oaks screened the pool off nicely from the road. Over at the table-tennis table under the apple-trees he could see the girl's lilac-coloured top as she moved, her slim body dappled with shadow. She was wearing shorts. Her arms and legs were still pale, almost pasty. Attractive, though. Slim. That dark blond hair you never really see much except in England. Jack seemed to have taken a shine to her, anyway, and you couldn't blame him. That rather bland,

English sort of good looks could be an asset sometimes. Like with Liz when she was young – people had actually turned their heads to look at them as they came in, the young man with his full head of sandy hair, the tall fair girl on his arm. It wasn't until you had a few years of meetings and presentations and corporate team-building under your belt that you began to want out of all that. And then, right on cue, they came up with a really good offer, an early retirement package so good you actually couldn't refuse. And that was when it came to you suddenly – what you wanted was paradise on earth – no more, no less. And the surprising thing was that it was attainable, it was there for the taking, if you only had the gumption just to open your two hands as wide as you possibly could and grab.

He rubbed the worst of the wetness away with the towel and lowered himself on to the lounger again, this time on his front, his cheek resting on his arms. His skin was cool now and smelled of the water. *All this* . . . He was so lucky. He let himself sink, smiling, into the soft red darkness at the back of his own eyes. From the open gable window of the house he could just hear Lizzie's digital radio, tuned to a British station. The ping-pong ball stopped ticking backwards and forwards and the two young voices under the apple-trees sank to a murmur, twining gently in and out. All this. The lovely old French house with its deep window-recesses and ancient stone walls and that wonderful crooked roof ridged with terracotta tiles. The virginia creeper waving round the doorway, that would turn a brilliant, unbelievable red every September. The stone-flagged kitchen with a table big enough to seat a family of twelve. The big, gaping garage-barn with its rickety ladder still leading up to that circular window – an ox-eye window, they called it – and what had obviously once been the hay-loft. The orchard. The poolside patio and barbecue, where you could have the kind of summer parties you never even dreamed about in your youth. *It was all his.* Until they'd seen it, until that English bloke over in Champfleury had actually mapped out the pool to scale and written in the dimensions and shown him the designs, he wouldn't have believed it possible. Not in real life. It was the kind of thing his own father would have goggled at in disbelief, the kind of asset that would make even his old colleagues glance at him slyly and say, 'Pete, where did all this come from, you jammy sod?'

He winced as somewhere deep in his body a muscle seemed to tighten of its own accord. He concentrated on relaxing – his face, his fingers and toes, his calves, the knotted mass of his neck and shoulders. If he could let himself go enough and not fight, it was hardly noticeable, just a dull ache in his bowels somewhere. If he concentrated he could almost make it disappear entirely. And then the sunlit garden was just as it had been before, the blue water of the pool lapping gently at the overflow with a little sucking sound almost under his bare feet.

He breathed in slowly. One, two, three . . . Better. He breathed out, and already the feeling had passed. It was nothing. It was hardly noticeable; perhaps he'd imagined it entirely. And it wasn't as if it happened very often. Once a month, at most. Or once a fortnight, anyway. Usually it would wake him in the night and he'd get up and go to the bathroom and lie down again and after a minute or two it would recede. Or he'd notice it when he was out walking, sometimes. And once it'd got him just when he was talking

39

to that MacLaren chap about a chipped tile on the nose of one of the dolphins, he'd had to stop himself from doubling up with the sudden unexpected sting of it, and afterwards, when MacLaren left and he'd gone inside, his underpants – he could hardly even think of it – had been soiled with something that was almost certainly just a touch of indigestion, something he'd eaten at that restaurant in Mirlac the night before, a bit too much olive oil – certainly nothing as worrying or complicated as blood.

But there was no getting away from it. Even now, wrapped in this sweet air and sunlight, he could sense it somewhere just out of range. As long as he relaxed . . . As long as it stayed the same, he could just lie here breathing quietly and concentrate on smoothing it away. He could feel it now, just at the edge of consciousness, coiling, taking shape slowly in the pit of his body and rising in a slow spiral, showing its flicker of tongue. But he could breathe it away. He could simply lie here without moving a muscle, and gradually the almost-ache would curl back on itself and melt into the walls of his body, disappearing the way it had come.

In spite of everything, Lizzie was still quite presentable in her tennis outfit. True, she'd never achieve that French look – all smooth brown skin and downturned smile and something teasing in the eyes. But the short skirt flattered her all the same. She didn't have protruding veins in her legs like some women her age. And she was useful on court. She still had a pretty mean backhand sometimes. She enjoyed it, you could tell. The pleasure of running around shone out of her, even if she did drive him mad occasionally with her fond reminiscences of improbably green grass courts back in

England. He didn't mind it, usually. It was just today, after dropping that Alex girl off in Champfleury. After having to rouse himself against his inclinations from his perfect afternoon by the pool.

They were playing doubles, with a young French couple called Jean-Yves and Chloë. He could just see the woman at the far end, rocking on her expensive tennis shoes and passing her racquet from one hand to the other as if she fancied herself some kind of pro. He braced himself and sent his first serve straight down towards her. She didn't react fast enough and the ball bounced off the frame of her racquet into the air. He heard her distant yelp. He walked over to the other side of the court, and did the same again.

He played brilliantly. It was almost a whitewash. Only one or twice did his concentration lapse slightly, allowing the young French couple to take a couple of easy games. Liz hardly had to do anything. At the end he zipped up his holdall and made straight for the car, barely stopping to shake hands.

'Well, that was pretty convincing.' Liz put her bag in next to his and went to stand over by the left side of the car.

He closed the boot with a slam. 'Are you driving?'

'No, I . . .' She blushed as she realised her mistake. She walked round to the passenger door and stood for a moment with her face turned to the glitter of the poplar trees on the other side of the clubhouse. Even now she hardly ever remembered. Especially when she claimed she was tired or had something on her mind.

He deactivated the central locking and slid into the driver's seat. The air in the closed car was almost unbreathable, the steering-wheel too hot to touch. She got in beside him without speaking. He reached for the button on the dashboard and something dry and warm blew into their faces, growing cooler almost at once. 'What do you mean, "convincing"?' he said.

'You massacred her.'

'I didn't.'

'Yes you did. I saw her face.'

He touched the wheel cautiously with the tips of his fingers. It was just about bearable. He let in the clutch smoothly and the car eased forwards out of the car-park and down the drive, following the long curve. Across the fields he could see the Taux, its near bank marked by a line of willows. Even in June, they looked dusty. 'Aren't you supposed to beat your opponents?' he said. 'I thought that was the whole point.'

'Watch out!' A grey Peugeot was turning into the drive too fast, almost clipping their wing-mirror.

'Get over!' Pete turned the wheel sharply and they jerked to a halt at the junction. He looked in both directions with exaggerated caution. 'Stupid arsehole. What did he think he was playing at?'

She said, 'It was Jim MacLaren. With . . .'

'I don't give a fuck who it was.'

She turned to glance at him. 'What's the matter with you today? You demolished that poor woman on the court just now. She was almost in tears, didn't you notice? And why were you so rude to Alex this afternoon when you dropped her off? Couldn't you see Jack really liked her? And she seemed pretty keen as well. She looked so forlorn when she first arrived – it can't be much fun over there just with Susie and the baby in that run-down old place. And this afternoon she seemed really *happy*. They both did. She and Jack were really hitting it off. Didn't you see them? And then you come and put your big feet in it, shouting at her to get out of the car and now she probably thinks you're a great bully and they won't ever want to see each other again.'

He turned his head to stare at her. What kind of world did she live in?

But she hadn't finished. 'Are you jealous, is that what it is? Are you actually jealous of your own son?'

He wanted to laugh. She'd gone red, the freckles and sunburn blending together in one hectic blur.

Her mouth was still opening and closing, as if by some hidden mechanism. 'What's the matter with you lately? You kept saying this was all you wanted, that we were so lucky, that this was paradise . . .'

'It is.' Behind them in the mirror the poplars shimmered. He winced in the glare from the surface of the road. 'Can you pass me my sun-glasses?'

She gave a little movement of impatience and leaned forward to open the glove-compartment. She was feeling inside for the leather case. He heard her snap it open. She held the glasses out to him with the side-pieces already spread, and he took them with his right hand. ' "Thank you, darling",' she said.

He couldn't be bothered to reply.

He could feel her still looking at him, her eyes burning into his profile. 'So tell me,' she said. 'Why aren't you happier?'

'I am happy.'

She started to speak slowly, carefully. He could feel her choosing the words. 'I know it's a bit of a balancing act, England and our life over here. Swings and roundabouts. I know there must be things and people you miss—'

43

He took his eyes off the road to glance at her. '*Me?* I don't miss anything. England can sink into the North Sea for all I care.'

He felt her wince. She turned away from him, towards the window. They were skirting Champfleury now, past that row of old cottages. A parked car seemed to come suddenly out of nowhere, and he had to swerve to avoid it. That crazy taxi-driver. Why did he always have to park the thing there, just on the bend? Then they were passing the playground. Out of the corner of his eye he could see the swings, the pilgrim shelter with its laminated map and directions, the barbecue area with its little pile of rocks over to one side. He said, 'That thing's an eyesore.'

'What thing?'

'That hut thing. They ought to pull it down.'

'It's for pilgrims.'

'What pilgrims?' Even with the sunglasses, the sun was shining right in his eyes. He pulled down his sun-visor and she followed suit. He caught a flash of silver from her mirror as she lowered her hand. 'Have you ever seen any pilgrims there? I haven't.'

'You do see people sometimes – with hiking boots and rucksacks. Sometimes they leave their water-bottles behind.'

'They're not pilgrims, they're just walkers. And what is a pilgrim anyway? No one believes in all that stuff.'

'Some people do.' She was twisting her fingers in her lap. 'Here they do. Sometimes.'

'What do they look like, then? Tell me.'

'They have hats.' He could feel the tightness in her voice. She'd lose patience with him in a minute. 'Sometimes they have a scallop shell, a *coquille Saint Jacques*. Saint Jacques, for

44

Santiago, get it?' Her French accent was as bad as his, even after all this time.

'Do they really.' They were through the village now. A sign loomed at them at the side of the road, the name Champfleury crossed through with a red line. 'And what about you personally? Have you ever seen a pilgrim?' He heard himself speaking, his voice completely unlike itself. It might have been coming from someone else, or across an almost immeasurable distance. He could hear himself shouting at her. 'Well, have you?'

She said quietly, 'I am a pilgrim.'

Had he heard her right? But she did say these weird things sometimes. Perhaps this life – this missing their old life back in England – was getting to her. He yanked at the wheel in exasperation, and the tyres spun on the gravel as they turned sharply and accelerated up the hill towards Seyrac. He could just make out the long, low roof of Les Vergers on the hillside, the mellow colours of the old tiles through the trees.

It wasn't until bed-time that he realised he'd forgotten to put the cover on the pool. Liz was already in bed, watching satellite TV – some gardening programme from England, one of those things where a team of jolly, energetic people came while you were out at work and transformed your suburban patch into an unlikely landscape of cedar decking and water features and ornamental shrubs. He went outside and made his way towards the roll of steel rods and white nylon sheeting at the far end.

But something was moving. He jumped. Something in the pool was making slow ripples, in a regular movement that sounded like someone breathing. He ran back to the house and turned on the underwater lighting and the surface of the pool seemed to leap towards him, a gash of turquoise, making him blink.

'Thanks, Dad.' Jack rolled over in the water and floated face upwards, his feet breaking the surface with a small splash.

'It's you, is it? I thought it was one of the holiday lets. It's against the rules without the lights, you know that.'

Jack hauled himself out and sat on the side, dangling his legs in the water. Under him one of the dolphins rippled slightly. 'I thought you'd gone to bed and left the cover off. And it was just me.' He grinned through his wet hair. In this light it looked black. 'I didn't think anyone'd even notice.'

'You gave me a fright. I thought you were some animal and I was going to have to rescue you with the net.'

'One of the summer tenants, more likely.' Jack's skin had a bluish tinge. 'How was it this afternoon? Did you have a good game?'

'Not bad.' Pete slipped off his sandals. He bent down and rolled up the legs of his trousers, then lowered himself to the edge and let his feet hang in the water. He spread his toes and felt the coolness slip between them, smoothing into the cracks. 'How about you?'

'Me?' Jack laughed. 'Oh, you mean the ping-pong. Alex is great. I really like her. She's got this killer topspin thing she does.'

Pete swung his legs gently backwards and forwards. The dolphins shivered and disappeared. 'I'm sorry,' he said.

Jack's blue face looked puzzled. 'What for?'

'For shouting at her. Your mother told me I was rude.'

'I didn't notice.'

For a moment they sat together in silence. Pete said, 'Are

you seeing her again?'

'I don't know. Probably.'

'Good,' Pete said. But the word was lost. Below him a sudden splash rocked the water from end to end. At his side a heart-shaped patch of wet showed where Jack had just been sitting. A moment later a head surfaced. His son was on the far side of the pool, out of his depth, treading water. He raised a hand and beckoned. 'You should come in.'

'Shall I?'

'Why not? It's great.'

He stood up and pulled off his clothes quickly, draping them over the back of one of the plastic chairs. From the shallow end he eased himself in a step at a time, the water mounting slowly to his knees, his hips, his belly, swirling between his open fingers as he moved his arms. Then he lunged forward, opening the cold with his breast and his joined hands. 'Brrr!'

'Good?'

'Not bad.' The two of them were treading water side by side. Something caught between his fingers – a leaf? an insect? – and he threw it away from him towards the grass with a reflex of disgust. But the water was warmer now. It stroked his limbs like silk. He turned and struck out hand over hand towards the far end.

And then everything suddenly went dark. What the . . . ? For a moment he couldn't see even his own arms. Behind him he heard another splash.

He could feel Jack behind him, the water churning. Some-one's hands were on his shoulders, pushing him under. He went down to the bottom in a rush of black, feeling the bubbles of his own breath brushing the skin of his face as they escaped towards the surface. He came up, choking. 'You . . . !'

Beside him Jack was laughing.

He snorted. The inside of his nose stung. He could feel the strings of snot still dangling from his nostrils and he brushed them away with the back of his wet hand. 'You bloody swine!'

'What do you mean? All I did was—'

'You wait!' Pete stopped coughing and rolled over on his back. The world was beginning to show itself now. He could just about make out where the water ended and the paving began. Against the darkness of the sky that patch of denser darkness must be the umbrella, and beyond it the trees. As he went on looking the differences seemed to get sharper. After a while the plastic furniture had a sort of pale glow about it. He could see the whites of Jack's eyes.

And then the stars came out, a peppering of whiteness in the dark blue. Low down, a planet glittered almost orange. Single stars like tiny rips in the fabric. And the brightest in each small cluster surrounded itself with a kind of milky dust, like a fingerprint, or the tail of a comet, as if something out there were moving past the earth almost impossibly fast. He said, 'You were right.'

'I know.'

'It's amazing.'

'Even if it is against the rules.' His son was laughing at him, he could hear it in his voice.

'Fuck the rules.'

Jack didn't answer. Surprised to hear him swear, probably. Pete could feel him treading water at his elbow.

Pete glanced at him out of the corner of his eye, before letting himself drift backwards, the nape of his neck immersed in cold. For a while they lay side by side on the surface, float-ing, part of the landscape of the sky. Then he started to feel dizzy and brought his body back to the vertical. 'Jack?'

'Mmm?'

'Go for it.'

'What?'

'You're young. Mum and I, we're . . .'

Jack reached for the side and turned in one smooth move-ment like a racer. A moment later Pete heard him surface two or three yards farther down. 'It's starting to freeze my balls off. Beat you to the end.' His voice was grinning. The ripples fanned out behind him as he swam in a leisurely breast-stroke towards the steps, making a gentle lapping sound when they met the wall.

MAGALI

When she first sees him he's talking to someone. He's standing by the low wall with two strangers. He frowns as he tries to tell them something, pointing to the watch-face on his wrist.

She hangs back under the awning of the boulangerie at the corner of the rue des Menuisiers, where he can't see her. The guy's holding out money to him and he's taking it, folding the notes in half and stuffing them into the back pocket of his jeans. Then he's ushering them towards the gap in the wall where the old stone steps go down to the little quay underneath and a couple of canoes are tethered to an iron ring. After a while she crosses the rue du Taux and sits on the wall to watch. He's holding the boat steady with his foot while they get in – a boy with bright red hair she seems to half recognise, a girl she hasn't seen before. Obsessing about each other, obviously. She can see it in the way the boy's clinging on to the girl's wrist as she half-falls forward across the narrow gap. And in the girl's eyes as she looks back. They're not part of this place, somehow. Their eyes are too pale, their skin's too exposed to the sun. They settle themselves in the canoe, leaning forward over the brown water to take hold of the paddles. Then Théo gives them a little push with his toe and they nose out onto the quiet surface, their prow cutting a thin, clear line between the floating leaves.

It's at moments like this, when Théo's totally out on his own somewhere, that she can start to see him properly, start to get a sense of who he really is. He bends his head to check the knot that holds the second canoe to the rusted ring, and she wants to reach forward and run her fingers up through his hair. He walks towards the steps and stands there watching for a moment until the two English kids have disappeared behind the overhanging willows. She loves that small furrow at the back of his neck, where the short dark hair bends and springs back under her fingers like warm fur.

He looks up suddenly and sees her and his forehead crumples with surprise. He's squinting up at her through the sunlight, grinning. 'You managed to get away.'

'Just about. My precious mother wanted me to hang around and peel a load of apples. My uncle's coming over tomorrow, with all the little runts. I told her I had stuff to buy in town.'

'Like what?' He comes over to her and kisses her on both cheeks. The smell of his skin makes her feel slightly giddy. She leans into him for a moment, pushing her face into the warm valley of his shoulder, and he puts his arm round her and hugs her to his chest. Then he gives her a little push, so she almost loses her balance. 'Like a bicycle? Like a canoe?'

They sit down on the wall side by side and she reaches into her bag for the apple she filched from the pile this morning. With his penknife he cuts it cleanly in half – two white circles of perfect flesh. She watches as he bites into the green. She can hear him chewing, see his jaw-muscles moving under the skin. He eats it right down, turning to throw the core into the river with a flick of his brown arm. How does he do that? She hears the faint plop as it hits the surface, a long way over, somewhere in the shadow of the trees on the opposite bank. It's something about boys' bodies, and girls'. How must it feel to be able to send something flying from your hand like that, so easily and so far?

'For the fish,' he says. He goggles back at her until she moves away from him. He laughs.

She says, 'What time do you get off?'

'It depends. If no one else comes, it could be around 16.30. Can't go anyway till they come back.' He gestures with his head downstream.

She plays with the end of her belt, rolling and unrolling it in a stiff curl between her middle finger and the ball of her thumb. The metal eyelets are hot to the touch. 'When *are* they coming back?'

'In a couple of hours.'

Two hours is quite a long time. You can do quite a lot in two hours. She lets go of the belt and picks up his hand. The inside of his palm is slightly damp under her fingers. 'Then can't we . . . ?'

'Are you crazy?' He slips his hand gently away from hers as if absent-mindedly. 'What if someone comes? They could shove the bikes in the back of a van and be halfway to Bordeaux or Toulouse before anyone even noticed. My Dad would go spare.'

She stands up and pulls him to his feet beside her. She takes hold of his two hands and joins them behind her back, leaning in to his body. 'Do you think anyone will come?' She pulls his face down to hers and runs the tip of her tongue along his upper lip. She breathes into his ear, 'Would anyone even really notice you'd gone?'

But he yanks his face away from hers and takes a step backwards and she lets her arms fall to her sides. She can feel herself standing stiffly, her shoulders hunched. 'What's the matter?' Listen to her. She sounds like she's trying to start a quarrel. 'Are you going to do what he tells you for ever? You're seventeen!'

He's avoiding making eye contact. The toe of his grimy trainer makes a line, up and down in the dirt. 'Look. He's doing his thing in the café. Mum's working her arse off. What do you expect? They need me. I can't just decide to take a few hours out whenever I feel like it. Someone might come along just at that moment.'

'And stomp off up to the café demanding to know how the son of the family could have betrayed his father's trust.'

'That's not what I meant. I wasn't thinking about me. I was just thinking we'd lose the custom, that's all.'

'And where would we be without our customers?' She hears her voice saying it, hard as her mother's, and winces. 'All those good city-dwellers on holiday enjoying themselves. The Rosbifs. The Frites-Mayonnaise. The Clogs. Let them fuck off, the lot of them. Can't you ever just do what you want?'

'I will be doing what I want soon.' He looks suddenly serious. She can hear the quiet determination in his voice.

'Yeah?'

'I'm not going back to school. I've decided. I don't have to go on living here with them. Your brother left, and there wasn't a thing your mum could do about it. A few more weeks and I'm out of here. I'm going to start up on my own.'

'That's wonderful.' She can't keep the sarcasm out of her

voice. 'That's just fantastic. And what are you thinking of using for cash?'

'I'll work in a shop or as a waiter or something and do my own thing on the side. On the edge of a big town. Toulouse. Or Montpelier. A few bikes, that's all it takes. Build it up slowly. Things gradually getting better. The bikes getting newer every season till you hardly even have to oil them once in twelve months and check the brakes. A couple of years and I'll be into mountain-bikes, racing-bikes... I could have my own shop.'

His face and body are alive as he talks about it, his eyes full of suppressed excitement, his brown hands drawing it all for her in the air. He could be miles away already, a speck getting smaller on a dusty road. She says, 'Great.'

She glimpses the sideways gleam of his eyes as he says, 'I may carry a few ladies' bikes as well, if there's any demand.'

She punches him, and he catches her arm and kisses her suddenly. His fingers hold her gently behind her ears as his tongue enters her, warm and slippery, filling her mouth till she can't feel or think about anything else. The sky, the river, the reflected trees seem to disappear. She's all only warm wet breath and sliding, shivering touch. It's like when she was a child, when she used to wake up in the night and everything was completely dark and she used to wonder if she'd suddenly gone blind. Her legs are turning to liquid so she can hardly stand. She leans against him and he runs his hands over her face, still kissing her, his breath in her nostrils and against her cheek. Then there's a crash and they jump apart, the world spinning round them like faces glimpsed from a roundabout, their fairground horse still rising and falling on its barley-sugar pole. One of the bikes is lying at their feet, its handlebars twisted, its back wheel turning gently over the dry dirt.

When the two English kids come back she finds herself looking at them half-enviously. Where have they been, in their battered rented canoe? Did they moor somewhere under a tree and lie on the shady bank looking up at the sun glittering in the leaves? Have they had sex? They look relaxed enough, the girl's smile somehow secretive, the boy's hand on her back as she steps out onto the quay almost tender. Her clothes are more crumpled than they were; his T-shirt's dark with sweat under the arms and in the small of his back. The girl's face is slightly burnt, as if she's been lying back in her seat while he worked above her, paddling the canoe forward alone. But still you get this feeling there's something important between them – something more than sex – as if they've both been travelling in a foreign country and bumped into each other by chance and realised they spoke the same almost forgotten local dialect. As if he showed her a map of where he built a camp in the woods when he was a small boy and she looked at it and said, *Yes, that's where I buried my heart.*

How sentimental is that? Magali shakes herself. God! There's sex, and there's the other thing – families crowded together in their small houses, her mother thick-waisted and embarrassing in that grotesque navy and yellow house-dress, screaming at the boys to clear up in the yard as she stirs the soup. But the thought comes back to her again as they make their way up the rue des Menuisiers towards the café: the boy cutting his way along the overgrown path, the girl's heart waiting in its perfect casket as if for this moment, the branches criss-crossing as if no one's been that way for a hundred years.

She's still thinking of them as she ducks through the curtain of plastic ribbons. Maurisse is standing over by the cash register, talking to one of the customers, his thick arms spread across the counter, sleeves rolled up. She looks round for Jeannine, but there's no sign of her: she must be somewhere out at the back – in the kitchen making dinner, or folding up sheets and towels from one of the lines strung across to the big plane tree behind. Maurisse looks up at them, registering her presence. He nods and she meets his eyes. 'Not working?' he says to her.

It's too complicated to go into – her mother's hopes for her, her own unspoken plans to go to the University, the way she can't seem to get herself organised this summer. All her friends have holiday jobs. She shakes her head.

'So you've been giving Théo a hand.' He pulls a beer slowly, letting the foam run down through the grating, and wipes his fingers on the bib of his apron. '*Voilà.*' He puts the glass down with an exaggerated flourish. What a pompous idiot! 'It's nice for him to have a friend.'

She hears herself say, 'Théo's got lots of friends.'

'But not all of them come and help him when he's at work.' Maurisse looks at her meaningfully. She isn't sure whether he's approving or disapproving. 'It's good, a companion when you're working. Look at me. Look at this.' He gestures theatrically at the lines of tables under their red-checked oilcloth and the few customers glance up at him in amusement or alarm. 'I couldn't have done any of it without Jeannine.'

'No.' It's hard to meet his eyes. He's a caricature. The idiotic moustache makes her want to laugh.

He says, 'And I'm not as young as I was.' The way he

spreads out his fingers is slightly theatrical. He's rehearsed this whole speech many times. 'It's not a pleasure-trip, a café, I don't have to tell you. Especially with the other business to keep up as well.' He points with his head towards the door. 'When you're young you don't really have any conception. Théo thinks it all just looks after itself. But it takes at least two to run a place like this.' He crosses his arms across his chest and she can see the hairs, dark as fur and all pointing in the same direction.

She nods. She can feel Théo behind her. She can almost sense the tension in his body, the set of his mouth. Why doesn't he say something to rescue her? But he only leans across her to pick up a paperback that's lying face downwards on the counter. It looks like some kids' book – dog-eared and grubby, the cover streaked white with creases. 'What's this?' He runs his hand over the battered cover.

Maurisse gives a short laugh. 'Oh, someone just left it behind. Those two old geezers that come in here sometimes for an apéritif. That old schoolteacher and his mate. Sit at that table over in the corner. Know the ones I mean?'

'Yeah, I think so. Doesn't he live out in Champfleury?' Théo turns towards her. 'He probably taught you.'

'Monsieur Briot?'

'That's the one.'

She reaches out for the book and leafs through the pages. It seems to be something to do with the Second World War.

'Take it,' Maurisse says. 'Read it if you want to. They won't notice. They won't even be in here again for another couple of weeks.'

'Okay, I will. Thanks.' She smooths the corners of the pages and closes the old paperback gently. Behind him Jeannine appears in the kitchen doorway, her hair sticking to her cheeks in little wisps. Christ! They're all closing in, like dogs crashing through the undergrowth, scenting blood! Magali holds out her hand. 'Actually, I've got to get back.'

'Already?' Maurisse's voice is so loud it makes her jump. A couple of the customers exchange glances. 'But it's early! You haven't even had anything to drink. You must be dying of thirst. What can I offer you?' The corners of his eyes crinkle in a way that reminds her suddenly of Théo.

She shakes her head.

'Are you sure? Jeannine, she says she's leaving. Are you certain you won't have something – a grenadine, a little lemonade?'

She can feel the blood rising to her face. 'Really. I promised to help my mother this evening. I've got to go.'

'What a good girl! She helps her mother.' Old Maurisse looks across at Jeannine and winks, his moustache moving slightly as if he's about to break into song.

'Leave her alone, Dad,' Théo says. 'She'll think you're completely bonkers. Didn't you hear what she said?'

They shake her hand and she walks away from them backwards, watching their big faces recede. Théo accompanies her to the doorway and they give each other a quick kiss on both cheeks. He holds her for a moment, his face pressed against her own, and she closes her eyes, feeling his ribs expanding as he breathes.

She walks back along the pilgrim path. It could be any old footpath, leading from anywhere to anywhere. She's been this way so often and she hardly ever meets anyone. It's always been there, ever since she can remember. Even when she was tiny she always knew what the red and white markings meant, the L-shaped flash on a rock or a tree-trunk where you had to turn suddenly left or right, the crosses at junctions to tell you you were about to go wrong. It's just a path like any long-distance path, joining the dots of towns and villages, leading southwest towards the Spanish border, or south in a little rocky detour that takes you down through Lourdes. You hardly ever meet anyone walking, in either direction. Yet she's aware of taking it against the flow. As a child she'd come this way – sometimes on her own and sometimes with one or other of her brothers – into town and then back with a bunch of wild flowers or a few rectangles of chocolate and a *ficelle*, stopping sometimes under a tree to eat. Her mum never minded, never even seemed to have time to worry about where she was. It was M. Briot who looked after them all really. He was the only one who seemed to care about who they were and what they might become.

Funny old guy. She remembers him moving among them from desk to desk, his hair grey even then, his head bent over a child's smudged map or drawing or page of messy sums. How he'd say, 'Good. Good,' and give you a sort of quizzical look. And suddenly you'd see what you'd done wrong and rub it out and everything would start coming together. He'd point with the tip of his pencil to something on the page and tap the lead gently against the paper and say, 'And what about this bit? Have you thought about what you might be able to do with this?'

Her eyes fill with tears. Crazy. What a lovely man he was! And he still reads kids' books, even now he's retired. And works in the village post office now a couple of hours a day, of course – she's been in there once or twice, standing in

front of him completely tongue-tied, as if she was still about
six and holding out her hands to be inspected before lunch.
A bird flies up suddenly from the edge of a cornfield, making
her jump. God! What on earth was that? A skylark? He used
to show them pictures of birds and animals sometimes and
try and make them learn their names. *Alouette* . . . Such a funny
man really. Not a bit like most people round here. So low-
key. So patient. She catches herself wondering what his life's
like without all the children, what he's found to keep himself
busy, whether he ever thinks about them now.

One evening she brings Théo out this way. The path isn't
wide enough for the two of them to walk abreast and he lets
her go in front, pushing past weeds and under overhanging
branches. She holds a trailing bramble aside for him while he
ducks under her hand. When they stop her shoe-laces are full
of grass-seeds. She bends down to pick them out. He goes to
light a cigarette, but she puts her hand on his arm.

He looks as her in surprise. 'Why not?'

'It spoils things.'

'What things?'

'I don't know. The place.'

'What do you mean, 'the place'? What's the matter with
a quick fag, for God's sake? It doesn't do anyone any harm.'
He lights up anyway, shaking the match out with a flick of
his wrist. He's striding in front now. She follows his thread
of smoke as it hangs between the leaves.

Just off the pilgrim route there's a small side-path that
leads into the woods. There's a hide the local huntsmen use to
shoot from when the wild pigeons go over in the spring. It's
like a tree-house up there in the branches of a big chestnut.

She follows him as he shins up the rough ladder to the door.
It's fastened with a rusty padlock. Théo leans across and
puts his weight on a branch so he can swing himself up and
in through the glassless window. 'Here. Put your hand here.
That's right. Lean on me. That's it. There you go.' He swings
her in across the sill and sets her on her feet gently. It isn't
bad. Not too damp at all. A dim green light shines into the
corners. She picks up a piece of dead twig and brushes the
worst of the leaves and pine-needles and droppings into a pile
on one side. She's incredible thirsty suddenly. She takes the
bottle of Vittel from her belt and upends it between her lips so
the water runs into her mouth and down her chin. It's warm.
She wipes her mouth with the back of her hand and passes
the bottle to him without speaking and he drinks down the
rest, his adam's apple moving up and down under the skin.
She puts her hand up to feel it and he draws back, spluttering.
'Are you trying to choke me or what?'

'What.'

'I thought so.' He pulls her towards him, slipping his hand
under her T-shirt and moving it across her bare midriff. She
shivers. She can feel the familiar dizziness starting, turning
her legs to water, blurring her vision till the window's a
square of wet light swimming with leaves. His mouth is next
to her ear. He says suddenly, 'Have you done this before?'

The world slips back into focus. She blinks. 'Come to this
hide, you mean?'

'Or somewhere else? With someone else?'

She doesn't answer. She pulls him down to the floor. She
feels herself expanding under his fingers, her body getting
larger, the pores of her skin opening and breathing. Her
fingers and toes spread like petals, her breasts and belly swell

like fruit to meet his hands. And then she's huge, her thighs are touching the walls, pressing against the green air outside. And somewhere he's in there with her, his brown hands all over her and outside the trees whispering, like rain, leaf-shadows moving across her in the half-light from the little window, leaving their small green skeletons all over her skin.

By the time they walk home it's almost dusk. In one place it's too dark to see the path and they cut through into a vineyard to make the going easier. The rows of vines slope down the hillside towards them, fanning out at their near ends into the spokes of a huge wheel. He's holding her hand, swinging her arm lightly as they walk. He says, 'When we get to Toulouse we'll be able to do it in a bed.'

'Or on the saddle of one of your bikes.' She snorts with laughter. Calm down. He'll think you're crazy. But it's stronger than she is. She hears herself say, 'A tandem, perhaps.'

He stops walking and turns to face her. He touches the side of her face. 'Do you ever manage to be serious?'

'Sometimes.'

He hesitates. 'Are you serious about me?'

The earth at their feet's uneven, hard to stand on. She almost loses her balance and topples against him, putting out a hand to save herself. He folds his arms round her and they stand there together without moving for a moment in the half-darkness. A cricket chirrs and another one answers it, somewhere over towards the edge of the field. 'Well, are you?' he asks her again.

Her neck's hurting, her head pressed uncomfortably against his shoulder. She moves it slightly.

She feels him recoil. 'You've had other guys.'

What should she say? Should she deny it? But what's the point. She wants to be honest with him, to be herself. She says, 'Does it matter?'

He releases her and they start walking again, stumbling in the dried ruts left by the tall tractor, his arm round her shoulders. They keep falling against each other or knocking against each other's elbows or knees. He says, 'So will you?'

'Will I what?'

'Come to Toulouse with me.'

'Théo, listen.'

Above the hill a sliver of new moon is a white nail-paring. But he hasn't waited to hear her answer. She looks round for him but he's not at her side any more, he's off somewhere up near the rows of vines. She sees his dark shape staggering back towards her across the uneven ground. He's holding something out.

'What is it?'

'Gently.'

She takes it from him with two hands, not daring to close her fingers. Something soft and slightly velvety brushes against her palms. A moth? But something pricks her on the finger. It's a rose. He flings himself to his knees at her feet. 'Marry me.' Okay, he's laughing, he's decided the way out of this is to make a complete clown of himself. But he's serious. She can still hear the hint of real tension behind his voice.

'Are you completely out of your mind?' She turns and starts to walk quickly away from him, towards home.

He's running to catch up. She can hear his feet just behind her. He's shouting something after her but he's panting and she can hardly make out what he's saying. She stands and waits for him, holding the flower upright like a sword in front of her nose.

It's almost completely dark now. When he comes to a halt all she can see are the whites of his eyes. She says, 'You know what this is, don't you?'

He doesn't say anything. He's waiting for her to tell him.

'You know why old Vandrech plants them here. When it dies it means something's really wrong. When it withers or gets greenfly or phylloxera or whatever.'

'Do roses get phylloxera?'

She doesn't answer him. She says, 'What do you actually see us both doing in Toulouse?'

The outline of his face changes slightly as he frowns. 'What do you mean? I'd get some kind of job, just till we'd got enough to start the business, I told you. And you could work with me too if you wanted. For a couple of years, anyway, just till we... you know... and then I might have to let you stay at home for a bit while I keep it all going on my own.'

She tries to make out his expression but it's impossible. Something that feels like an insect has settled on her leg, and she bends down to brush it off. It comes away in her fingers – a crumpled rose-petal, black in the darkness – she's been pulling them off one by one and scattering them without noticing what she was doing. 'Théo, have you really thought about all this? Why would we want to go to Toulouse, when your dad's got a perfectly good café and bike business here?'

'Are you saying you actually want to stay in this dead-and-alive hole?' She can hear the puzzlement in his voice.

She opens her eyes wide and lets the shadowy landscape fill them completely. The stars are coming out. She can see Venus low on the horizon. 'No. It isn't that.' Her voice comes out croaky and she swallows and tries again. 'It's just . . .'

What can she possibly say to him? He's got absolutely no idea of the ambitions she has for her own life.

'I get it,' he says. 'You're waiting for someone else to come along, someone who's not starting from scratch. You're waiting for a better offer.' They've joined the path again and walking's easier. He pushes on in front, a solid dark shape just ahead of her as she struggles to keep up. He's got his hands in his pockets, his shoulders slightly hunched.

'No. Théo. Wait! It isn't like that.' But he strides on ahead, not seeming to hear her. And it's weird – now she's panting to catch up with him she can actually smell the end-of-row roses, just a hint on the night air, richer and darker than the smell of the cooling earth.

SUSIE

She was just finishing the washing-up when she heard what sounded like a small truck drive into the yard. Damn him! It was the worst possible moment. Didn't he realise she'd got to go out in a minute? What time was her appointment with that American woman? Half past? She dried her hands on the sides of her dress and went to the front door.

Jim was just sliding out of the driver's seat, his head bent so his scalp shone through the hair where he was going thin on top. He straightened and stood for a moment looking up towards the gables without seeing her. Then he strode towards her across the gravel, not bothering to lock the door of the cab behind him, the keys swinging from his hand.

'You got my message.' She heard her own voice saying it. It sounded bright and false, embarrassing. 'You didn't actually have to come yourself. You could just have rung someone.'

He shrugged. 'I thought I might as well just have a quick look. Sometimes all it is is a bad connection, or the plug's not been pushed all the way in.'

He would say that. She walked awkwardly in front of him into the kitchen, feeling his eyes on her back. Over on the other side of the table Alex was giving Jade her lunch. The lower half of the baby's face was covered with something that looked like carrot. As soon as she saw Jim she started to bump up and down in the highchair, waving the spoon away. He leaned across and kissed a clean corner of her forehead, nodding to Alex as if they'd already been introduced – he must have seen her with Jack at Les Vergers. He went over to the washing-machine and squatted down in front of it, gazing into the clear plastic eye of the door as if he was trying to read the darkness inside.

'It can't be anything to do with the plug,' she said, 'or the rest of it wouldn't work. It still washes alright. It's only the spin that's gone.'

He didn't say anything. He pressed the door-catch button and reached inside the hole with his arm.

'What are you doing?'

He grunted, gripping the inside of the door-seal and pulling till the machine scraped forward a few inches over the uneven floor. She rushed to pull the plug out of the wall socket and he grinned up at her, one eyebrow raised. 'Nice to know you still care.' He gestured with his head towards the power socket. 'It's the brushes probably. Or the bearings. One or the other. Did you say it was noisy?'

She shook her head. The machine was out in the middle of the floor now, blocking Alex's path as she tried to move around with Jade's things, and before she could say anything he was half-lying on the tiles beside it, his forehead resting on its white-painted side. He wriggled a screwdriver out of the pocket of his jeans. 'Don't even think about it,' she said.

'For fuck's sake! I thought you wanted it put right!'

She glanced at Alex. 'I do.'

He frowned, raising himself on one elbow to loosen the

screws one by one. Then he stood and lifted the back away, propping it against the wall behind him. It was criss-crossed with cobwebs, filthy. He bent forward again, staring into the cave of the machine. 'Have you got a torch?'

She resisted the urge to get a damp cloth and sponge the cobwebs away. 'I can't get involved in all this now. I've got an appointment at the golf club at half past.'

He raised his eyebrow again. 'The golf club!'

She wouldn't react. She said, 'That's where I see some of my clients, remember?' She stood waiting as he lifted the panel back on and bent again to tighten the screws. She saw Alex looking in his direction, the cloth she was using to wipe Jade's mouth stopped in mid-air. The baby was fussing to be released from the highchair. Susie went over and lifted her out. Jade burrowed against her and she breathed in the clean baby smell, closing her eyes.

When she opened them Jim was dusting off his hands. She said, 'I've got to go.'

'Of course you have. You always fucking go.'

She felt the blood rush to her face. 'What do you mean?'

' "I have an appointment with a client".' He said it in a silly, simpering voice that was supposed to sound like a woman's – like her voice. 'You go, then. I'll ring up Miele this afternoon and get them to send someone.' He leaned against the front of the machine, trying to push it back into place, but something was catching underneath, the floor was too uneven. He let go and it fell forward on to its front feet with a crash.

She could feel the blood pumping behind her eyes. Did it show? Were they actually bloodshot? This was how it always was with him. He was always completely impossible. There was never any way to end it except by getting away. But Alex was already at her elbow, holding out her arms, and she bundled Jade across. She reached for her bag and in a moment she was on her own outside, squinting in the glare, the gravel crunching under her sandals. Her car was in the barn. She got in and waited for him to come and move the truck so she could reverse out and turn. Her hands were shaking on the steering-wheel, her dress sticking to her thighs. She wound down the window and tasted the sawdust-and-oil smell of the earth floor. She saw him in the doorway of the farmhouse. For a moment he was hidden by the body of the truck. Then his engine coughed and the first belch of diesel reached her, catching in the back of her throat.

As she set out her tools on the treatment-room table her hands were still shaking. Extra-soft moistening tissues; green aloe lotion; fleecy towels in toning shades of blue and green. She turned on the CD player and the room filled with music, a gentle twanging of foreign instruments she couldn't even put a name to. Or perhaps they produced it all in an electronic lab somewhere? *Music to Heal the Soul*, it was called. She closed her eyes briefly and saw a single spray of creamy orchids in a blue glass vase, a horizon of blue-forested hills, drops of blue water slipping through her fingers like time and yet never entirely ebbing away.

The American woman lay stretched out on the couch, wrapped in a white sheet. Through the folds you could just make out the slightly heavy curves of her body. Susie lifted the hem clear of the woman's toes. The left foot had patches of hard skin at the heel and under the big toe, the sole yellowed and flaking from wearing sandals. She didn't take care of her feet, obviously: she'd let herself get lazy with the nightly pumice-and-moisturising routine. Susie lifted the ankle and wrapped the whole foot gently in a towel. The right was only slightly better. She lowered it to the cushion and covered it. She realised she was holding her breath. *Relax.* God! What if the client noticed? But between the two green mounds of her feet the woman's eyes were turned towards the window. She seemed to be smiling.

Susie picked up her notepad and ballpoint and began on the questionnaire. 'How are you – in your general state of health, I mean? Are you perfectly well, or do you have aches and pains somewhere?' She knew the words by heart, varying them only slightly with each new client. 'We all lead such stressful lives nowadays.' She bit back a kind of hiccup. 'And what about diet? Fruit and vegetables? Brown rice? Pulses? You know, we're so lucky here with all the organic produce. Have you been to the little farmers' market at Aubrillac on a Sunday, under the old arcades?'

The woman answered briefly and the little boxes seemed to fill up with ticks of their own accord. Susie began to work on the woman's left foot, grasping it in both her hands and rotating it gently from the ankle, then kneading the sole lightly, squeezing the foot in on itself like a curling leaf. She picked up each toe one after the other and moved it in a small circle. 'You will tell me if the pressure's too hard or too soft?'

The woman didn't even seem to be listening. Her eyes were closed. She opened them with what looked like an effort. 'Excuse me?'

'If I'm pressing too hard and it's uncomfortable? You will let me know?'

'You bet.' The woman's face opened suddenly in a big

grin, taking Susie by surprise. The legs of the chair scraped on the tiles. 'If you hurt me I promise you'll be the first to hear about it.'

What an odd thing to say. Suzie felt for a point just under the ball of the second toe and pressed firmly with her thumb, watching the woman's face. Some obstruction there, obviously. Somewhere behind her the music tinkled. She moved her thumb slightly and pressed in again. The woman's eyelids flickered. 'How does that feel?'

'Perfect.'

She wasn't telling the truth – not the whole of it anyway. Susie could tell she'd found a sensitive point just by looking at the angle of the woman's foot on its bed of towel. Silly cow. She felt suddenly like standing up and taking her by the shoulders to give her a shake. What was the point of coming for therapy if you weren't going to enter into the spirit of it and do your bit? And why had she been so keen to make this appointment anyway? She probably didn't even believe in it. Could she possibly be some sort of spy? A journalist? A friend of Jim's? No. Don't go there. Her fingers felt weak again and she straightened her back for a moment. Outside the open window an old walnut-tree spread its arms to the afternoon sun. She took a deep breath. 'Laura, what is it you said you do?'

'I'm an educator.'

'I'm sorry?'

'I teach. In a University.'

'Oh,' Susie said. 'Right.' So that was it, then. No wonder. They did have problems sometimes, people like that, people who were in their own heads all the time and read too much. It was an odd kind of life, living everything through what you got second-hand in some library. In her mind's eye she was probably still sounding off to a lecture-theatre full of geeky students. 'Are you on holiday then?' Susie asked.

The woman's feet shook as she laughed. 'Sure. The semester's over. But as a matter of fact I'm on Sabbatical. I'm here for my research.'

'Research?' She felt herself frown. Did it have something to do with the power station? Or were there other scientific places around here, things she'd never heard of? Where they tested cosmetics on animals or made chemical weapons or something equally nasty?

'On a man called Gaston Philippe,' Laura said. 'Have you heard of him?'

Susie shook her head.

'He was from around here – Mirlac. Well, when I say from, I mean he spent his summers here. This was where he was raised. Where he did his best work too. Liked to wake up at five in the morning, apparently, and work till the middle of the afternoon, and then he'd hit the road, hiking the long-distance trail. Quite a life.'

'The pilgrim path?' Susie wrapped the left foot in towel and began working on the right. 'The one that cuts through the village?' Why would anyone would want to do that? Sometimes you saw them – the walkers or pilgrims or whatever – staggering in with their great heavy rucksacks in the early afternoons, when the sun was still high over the roofs. They came trudging up that last little hill, with the sweat all running down their faces. It wasn't her idea of fun. The man must have been a bit weird. She said, 'What kind of work?'

'What kind . . . ? Oh, writing. He was a writer.' There was a silence. Above the tree there was some sort of bird hovering over the first green – a kite, was it, or a hawk. It hung almost motionless, its wing-feathers fluttering ever so slightly. After a moment Laura raised herself on her elbows to look at her, her forehead creased with concern. 'Hey. Are you okay?'

The question snapped her awake. Her fingers had stopped moving and she pressed her knuckles into the sole of the foot again. God, how had she managed to get into this terrible conversation? Who cared? Some long-dead French eccentric. His books were sure to be unreadable. She said, 'What was he like?'

'Like?' Laura leaned back, stretching her neck against the pillow. 'Dedicated. Intelligent. Scrupulous. Used simple words to describe complex phenomena.'

'I meant . . . to look at?'

'Oh . . .' Laura shrugged and the towel unwound itself from her foot and slid to the floor. 'Not that charismatic, to be honest. Sort of austere? These thin lips.' She raised her head again to demonstrate and Susie wanted to laugh suddenly. Perhaps after all this American woman was basically all right. 'Used to wear a big hat,' Laura said.

'Did he . . . ?'

But Laura was still talking. It was a whole mini-lecture she was giving now on Gaston Philippe – his life, his habits, his writing. Susie bent her head and went on with the massage and waited for the flood of words to come to an end. 'So that's what I'm doing,' Laura said finally. 'I'm renting a cottage from a friend, just for the summer? She's called Andrea, you may know her.'

Susie felt her stomach muscles contract. She turned her face away, busying herself with her notes. The ballpoint pen slipped from her fingers and fell to the floor with a little clatter. It had rolled under the day-bed. She knelt down and stretched forward, her cheek almost touching the tiles. She could just manage to reach it and bring it back.

Laura said again, 'Are you okay?'

For God's sake! She steadied herself with her hand on the edge of the day-bed. If she wasn't careful she wouldn't even be able to read her notes when she looked at them again.

Laura said, 'She's British. She does something called E.F.L.'

' "E.F.L?" '

'English as a Foreign Language. She's been here a while. Started a relationship with some guy who makes pools. Maybe you've met.'

'I don't think so.' The air of the small room was close and sickly, the woman's feet sticking up in front of her face were too big, the skin on her soles flaking and yellow. The smell of the lotion made her want to gag. After a moment she realised all she could hear was silence. Something had happened to the CD and she hadn't even noticed. She went over to the player and pressed a couple of buttons quickly and the rippling music started up again. She stood with her back to the figure on the day-bed, breathing slowly in and out. That was better. Her hands weren't shaking so badly. The music surrounded her like blue water, taking her in, folding her in its gentle embrace. She could be on a boat, travelling to somewhere far away from this place, just she and Jade in a little cabin upholstered in rose-coloured silk. She concentrated on keeping her voice steady. 'I think I might have come across her once or twice.' Did that sound natural? *Breathe.* She closed her eyes for a moment. The blue trees, the icebergs with their cold blue hearts, slid smoothly past.

What was that all about? She tried to concentrate on driving gently along the little country roads. Another few minutes and she'd be in the outskirts of Aubrillac, swishing past the outlying garages and light industry and supermarket towards the market-place where people sat drinking at café terraces in dappled shadow. But that was almost a panic attack she'd had back there. How did that happen? How could she possibly be feeling this out of control when everything she stood for was about wellbeing and spiritual calm?

But that woman – Laura, her name was – she *was* a bit strange. A bit crazy to set up a therapy session when all she really wanted was just to talk about her 'research'. Research! She was probably one of those people who didn't even believe in healing – who just ran to their GP for a packet of pills. And yet . . . There was something about her that was interesting. She *had* noticed. She was just too tactful to ask what the matter was.

Susie turned the wheel sharply into the road that led up towards Mirlac. The tyres bounced in and out of the pot-holes, grass whispering along underneath the car. She saw the wiry body of a man walking ahead of her just before the bend. His loose, shabby jacket swung open as he plodded uphill. He stepped to one side to let her pass and she edged by, the car tipping sideways as its off-side wheels ran along the crest. Then she could see him getting smaller behind her in the mirror, his big hat cutting his face in half with its line of shadow. At the top of the hill there was a cluster of old buildings, some of them in their original state, some standing empty and almost in ruins, a few in the middle of being done up. Some of the dormer windows were boarded over; others were strung with cobwebs behind new glass. The barn door was a makeshift collection of nailed boards.

She picked up the letter from the dashboard and looked at the envelope again. Something from Jim's bank in England – why did they keep sending things to the old address? Probably just a circular about investment opportunities or insurance. What a joke! It was hopeless, all of it. His whole attitude. People called him generous and easy-going and a good bloke, but he was hopeless. Any money he had just seemed to evaporate somehow. But perhaps Andrea would be good for him, get him back on track. Perhaps . . . She felt her eyes prick again suddenly. God!

It was bad enough with that woman this afternoon. For a moment there she'd almost lost it. And perhaps the American woman – Laura – had even been aware of something. You didn't have to be a genius to notice when someone's whole life was falling apart.

What was it Jim had said to her that time, when she was expecting Jade? 'Do you call this living?' He'd stood in the bedroom doorway and bellowed it at her, so even old Didier and Murielle next door had probably got an earful. She'd gone over and shut the window and Jim had laughed into her face. He was drunk, she remembered that much. He'd been leaning against the door-frame, slightly unsteady on his feet, the glass still in his hand. He'd waved it at her, laughing. 'This pathetic little life of yours – running round after all these stupid women, all bored out of their tiny minds. What can you possibly get out of it? Do you even make enough to live on? I'd be surprised. It's just some fucking half-arsed girly hobby. You're just pretending to be alive.'

She hadn't realised that was how he felt. But perhaps it was the alcohol speaking. She said, 'And what you do is different?

What you do is so real?'

'They do actually end up with something, yeah.'

'You mean, my clients don't.'

He was sneering at her, his red face split by that scornful smile she'd come to know well in recent months. 'Not something you can see and lie down by and dip your fingers into, anyway. Not something you can swim in or take photos of to send your friends and family at home, with a mosaic on the bottom or state-of-the-art filters or underwater lights.'

She'd been desperate to sleep. The weight of her belly was making her back ache. She heard herself say, 'I'm sorry you find my little existence so pathetic. Perhaps you should go and find someone else, someone who earns a proper salary. Someone who can keep you in beer and spirits.'

'Good idea. Fucking brilliant!' He'd slammed the bedroom door and gone downstairs. She'd heard him tramp out to the barn and start the car. She hadn't even bothered to stop him. She'd heard the rasp of his tyres on the gravel as he screeched away.

She'd gone to bed then, dropping with tiredness, the baby inside her strangely quiet and still. She must have dozed. And a couple of hours later she'd heard the car come back. He closed the house door quietly and crept up the stairs, knocking against the walls and cursing under his breath. She turned her face to the window, pretending to be asleep as he undressed. But when he slipped in beside her he put his arms round her waist and kissed her gently on the back of her neck. He was cold, shivering. She could still smell the beer on his breath. But she turned to face him anyway. It was scary, this, for both of them. It sounded so wonderful: you walked out of your boring old routine in England and came down here to start a new life. The countryside was lush. The summers were long. The food and wine were amazing. Some of these half-derelict old properties were still cheap, compared to what you could get at home. But things could go badly wrong sometimes. You could have serious cash-flow problems, and be forced to sell. You could miss home more than you thought you would. Or everything could be perfect – the money coming in nicely, your social calendar busy with barbecues and tennis and winter video-parties – and you could still feel something missing at the centre of it all.

And then you were wide open to what felt like a kind of panic. What if his drinking got worse? What if he got really impossible to live with? What if you found yourself suddenly on your own with a small child? Or what if you just started to feel there was something wrong with all of it – this tumbledown old place, this driving round to other people's houses, the whole reflexology thing? What if it ended up just you and the baby, alone and drifting without food or water, out of sight of land? What if they discovered you floating on a raft somewhere burnt to a cinder with sores on your faces and then even when you seemed to get better the spirit inside you had somehow shrivelled up and died?

Died. In spite of the blaze of sun on the windscreen she shivered. Well, who knew what the future held? She pushed the letter into her pocket and slid out of the car, easing the damp cotton of her sundress from the backs of her thighs.

For a moment she stood blinking. It was so easy to forget how far you could see from up here – right across from one side of the valley to the other. The round cooling-towers at Jumelech made the villages under them look tiny. A plume of steam hung almost motionless over the left-hand tower like a fluffy little cloud. Between the plantations of poplar trees the river glinted and curled away out of sight. All this was what Jim and Andrea must be able to see from their terrace. She tried not to look towards the restored pink brickwork and pots of begonias. They'd got one of those French letter-boxes, a cream painted metal thing on a post, probably left there by the previous owner. Someone had even clipped on a red plastic clothes-peg for outgoing mail, the way the old people in the village did sometimes. How very quaint. She brushed against it accidentally with her hand as she slid her letter through the slot.

Over her shoulder a dog started barking suddenly. A woman's voice called out in English, 'Hello?' She looked round and saw Andrea standing there in cut-off jeans and a T-shirt. 'Susie?'

'There was a letter for Jim. It came the other day. I just . . .' She gestured towards the letter-box.

'Do you want to come in? We're out the back actually. Would you like a word with him?'

'No, no. It's okay.' She was backing away, towards the car. She felt behind her for the open door and pulled it wider. Under her foot something crunched and she looked down. It was the clothes-peg, one of its red plastic arms shorn off and lying in the dirt like a broken fingernail. She slid into her seat, the sweat running down her spine in what felt like a small river, soaking her underwear and the back of her dress. From somewhere over behind the house she heard a splash, the sound of voices talking and laughing around a pool.

ANDREA

It takes so little. A single step, a rush of air, a tiny increase of pressure. A burst capillary leaking into the brain. A small clot travelling slowly along an artery like a leaf in the gutter after a shower, snagging on something and travelling on, making its inexorable journey towards the heart. A life is that precarious. Somewhere over there in England her mother lies propped up on pillows, her left arm inert and unresponsive on the blue bedcover. She's following the movements of the nurses with a new, lopsided smile.

'So tell me, what do you think?' Laura's talking, pulling at her sleeve.

She tries to focus. They're standing in front of a fish-stall, the fish laid out in sheaves over ice with their flat eyes gazing up at the sky, the mouths slightly open. On one side, a heap of crayfish. The long antennae could almost be waving. They say you can hear them crying – or is that lobsters?

'Look at them,' Laura's saying. 'Aren't they neat?'

Neat? 'You can't send crayfish to the States,' Andrea says. 'How about one of those coloured baskets? You could pack it in bubble-wrap and post it. They don't cost much. Or a scarf. Perhaps she'd like a scarf?'

'Oh . . .' Laura opens her arms. 'It's so gorgeous! It's so French. I just want all of it!'

'Why don't you get a hamper? Fill it with goodies and stick it in your suitcase? It's big enough. If you throw out a few of those old books and notes you'll have plenty of room.'

Laura's arms drop to her sides abruptly. She's stopped laughing. 'I'm sorry, Andrea. I'm being selfish. And you have better ways of using your time. But, you know, you Europeans just have no conception of how . . .'

Oh God. Here we go. The culture bit. She finds herself staring at a display of cheeses, the *crottins de chèvre* all lined up on individual rush mats as if they were praying. And I'd pray too, if there were something I believed in. She has a sudden vision of her parents' little dining-room with the chrysanthemum curtains drawn, the ceramic marmalade-pot in the shape of a beehive and the little ceramic bees crawling all over it, her father spitting shreds of orange-peel into his fingers and lining them up along the edge of his plate.

'Or maybe soap?' Laura's stopped in front of a stall selling hand-made soaps. She picks one up and holds it under Andrea's nose. The trapped grains of lavender are like dead insects.

Andrea turns her head away. Around her the whole market's suddenly heaving – the bolts of coloured fabric, the espadrilles held together in pairs by rubber bands, the olives in every conceivable shade of black and brown and green and khaki, the printed tapestry canvases of nude women, the nectarines and apricots and lettuces and melons with their smooth, cool skins. Is she actually going to faint? But no. She takes a deep breath and the wave subsides.

'Watch out!' Laura reaches to warn her as she feels herself

jostled by a woman and almost stumbles. Something scratches the side of her leg. Laura's looking at her in concern. 'Are you okay?'

She moves out of the way. 'I'm fine.' Her voice as she says it seems to be coming from a great distance. 'I think I just need to sit down. How about that café on the corner? Don't worry about me. I'm perfectly all right.'

But it's good to sit down and let her eyes go out of focus, just watching the colours swim in and out of the dappled shade. After a while the people begin to come to life again. An old woman in a black dress and grey lisle stockings hobbles past them with a basket of shaggy oak-leaf lettuces. A little boy zigzags by without looking up, absorbed in a comic. A pair of elderly men approach from the other direction and sit down at the table next to their own. Out of the corner of her eye she sees one of them take a packet of cigarettes and a lighter from his jacket pocket and place it on the marble table in front of him. She hears him say something softly behind her. The other man answers with a short laugh. 'So tell me,' Laura's saying. 'I knew the moment I walked in, there has to be something wrong. Is it you and Jim?'

Even here under the trees the light's very bright. She's been too quick to push her sunglasses up into her hair. She pulls them down again. 'No. No. At least . . .'

Laura reaches for her hand on the table and she doesn't pull away. 'You can't fool me, Andrea. He still likes a drink, I couldn't help being aware of that.'

Andrea feels herself wince. Laura's always so direct. But she's never far wrong. Nothing new in that department. Even in a place like this you can't expect a miracle. But it's bloody hard to talk about. She closes her eyes and nods.

'And he's getting vindictive? Is that it?' Laura's stare's horribly piercing. It's a relief to be looking at it through the lenses of her sunglasses.

'No . . .' She brushes a dried seed from the table. 'There isn't anything I can put my finger on. He's a really good man.' Laura's forehead creases in a frown and she feels her own skin tighten. 'Honestly. You don't know him.'

'So what's the problem?'

Behind them one of the old geezers has lit up. She hears the sound of pouring and a plop as an ice-cube falls from the lip of the jug. 'It's not Jim, actually. Or not really. It's my mum. She's not at all well. I'm thinking about going back.'

'You mean, for good?'

'Good God no!' She almost laughs at the expression on Laura's face. What's the matter with her? Is she getting hysterical? 'Just for a while. A few weeks, or a few months. Perhaps not even that long.'

The young waiter's in no hurry to serve them. He seems preoccupied, standing with his back against the wall. Laura leans back in her chair, looking over her shoulder and waggling her fingers to catch his eye. Behind them one of the old boys has embarked on some seemingly interminable narrative, the elderly voice droning on and on, as if talking itself to sleep. She tries to listen, but she can't make out the words. If she turns a fraction she can just see them. They're hunched forward over their drinks, their heads close together, like two elderly schoolboys over some kind of mischief. Then the one who's been talking sits back and she almost gasps. In the morning sunlight his long thin head is a skull, the eye-sockets two deep holes of shadow. She feels Laura stroking her hand

and watching her intently. 'It's that bad?'

She doesn't answer. Her eyes are filling with tears. She shakes her head.

'Well,' Laura says. 'I guess you have to go visit. You just need to call the airline and buy a ticket.'

'I suppose so.' If it were only that easy . . . She has a momentary vision of those board cut-outs standing shoulder to shoulder at the roadside on the way to the airport. Two of them, both black, and featureless except for the bald statistic: *9 dead in 6 years*. A man and a woman, shoulder to shoulder. But her mother's going to get better, she tells herself. Her mother's life isn't just a number, to loom up and frighten people from the side of the road.

They sit for a few moments without speaking. The Orangina bottle feels rough and pleasantly cool under her hand. It'll be all right. She can fly over to England for a couple of weeks and it'll be a false alarm and her brother Will can take over and then she'll be back – a storm in a teacup. If Jim can just accept it and not . . . She watches Laura's throat moving as she drinks down her Perrier.

Laura smiles. 'Do you want to see what I bought?' She sticks her finger in her glass to extract the slice of lemon and sucks at the flesh. She flicks the crescent of rind into the glass ashtray.

'What? When?'

'Before you insisted on dragging me away from that wonderful cheese-stall. While you were so busy crashing into old women and wishing you were someplace else.'

'Sorry.' But what does she expect, for God's sake? I'm not a saint. She says, 'Go on, then. Show me.'

Laura rummages in what she calls her purse and puts

something down on the table in front of her. A paper bag.

Andrea unfolds it. She upends it gently and something small slides out into a little heap. 'Is it a bracelet?'

'A necklace.' Laura reaches across and spreads it across the marble surface. Little bronze-coloured charms, attached at regular intervals to a cheap-looking chain. 'Do you get it?' Why's she being so insistent? What is this? Laura's leaning forwards, looking at her. 'Don't you see what they are?'

'They're shells.' So bloody what? It's some touristy thing, the kind of junk they sell to kids in seaside gift shops. What on earth can have possessed Laura to want to buy something like that here?

Laura sees the expression on her face and laughs. 'Yeah, sure, they're shells. But *what kind*?'

She picks the necklace up and looks at it more closely. 'Scallop shells?' They're identical, fluted, as tiny as a baby's fingernails.

'And what do you call scallops in French?'

'*Coquilles Saint-Jacques?*'

'*Précisément.*'

She always thought Laura was a bit potty. What does it matter what kind of shells they are?

'*Saint-Jacques!* Santiago, get it? You're a linguist, I shouldn't have to tell you that. They're pilgrim shells! They're what you need to wear when you hike the trail – like Gaston Philippe. Didn't I tell you he used to go out hiking with a shell pinned to the front of his hat?'

She is crazy – completely bonkers. Andrea coughs. 'Right.' She slips the chain back into the mouth of the paper bag and pushes it across the table.

'It's for you,' Laura says.

'What?'

'It's a thank-you gift. I thought you could wear it when you fly back to see your mom.'

She can feel herself blushing. When she opens her mouth her voice sounds twice as English. She says, 'That's awfully nice of you, Laura. Thanks. I'm really touched.' Shit. Her voice is starting to shake. 'Though I haven't completely decided yet. I may be over-reacting. I haven't even told Jim. I've got to ring my brother in England. It may still be better to put it off for a bit.'

There's a little bird pecking at crumbs in the gravel. It's half-tame, so close it's almost between their feet. It stops and eyes them, its head on one side. Then it takes another hop forward. 'Don't,' Laura says.

Andrea waits.

'Don't put it off. You don't play around with those things. How many people do you have in your life who've loved you unconditionally? You need to say goodbye to her. If you wait around you could find you've lost your chance.'

As they drive back through Champfleury the clock strikes six. She says, 'It does that twice, have you noticed?'

'Excuse me?'

'The clock. It strikes the hour once. And then, a minute or so later, it strikes again.'

'Really?'

'Mm.' As they drive past the little playground something catches her eye and she glances sideways. There's some litter in the grass just in front of the shelter. The barbecue rocks are scattered and something like a drink-can flashes in the low sun. The season must be really beginning. Somewhere north

86

or east of here they've probably already started out, they're halfway along the path by now, the walkers or pilgrims or whatever. Another couple of weeks and they'll all start to come through.

'Why is that?'

She shrugs. 'I imagine it used to be for the people working in the fields. The first time was to make them look up from what they were doing and register the fact that an hour had gone by already. And the second time was so they could listen and count the strokes and realise how late it actually was.'

'A bit like what Gaston Philippe said about reading.' Laura's face is turned to the window. Her voice seems to be coming from a long way off. 'You read it once for the story, and then you read it again, to . . .'

Andrea waits for her to finish, but she leaves the sentence hanging. At a little triangle of grass they turn west, towards Mirlac. After a while the clustered roofs of Lermitte rise to meet them out of the green hillside. Andrea turns in between the old stone gateposts and switches off the engine. She reaches into the back of the car for her bag. As she walks up the path a spray of roses waves in front of her, almost brushing her face. She holds it to her nose, breathing in deeply. *Those old-fashioned pink ones we had growing in the hedge when I was a child. I'd almost forgotten what they smell like.* Behind her she hears Laura say, 'And which one is correct, the first time it strikes, or the last?'

Jim's sitting outside, at the table beside the pool, wearing a clean T-shirt over his swimming-trunks. There's a glass at his elbow. He sees her looking. 'Lemonade. I was thirsty.'

She nods. 'Have you just got back?'

'Yeah. I took Damien over to Susie's to fix the washing-machine. Dropped him in the village. Got in just before you did.'

She frowns. 'Damien? The taxi-driver? I thought you were going to ring the manufacturer.'

'He does all kinds of stuff. You'd be surprised.'

Behind the sunglasses her skin feels gritty. She takes them off and rubs at the corners of her eyes. 'Is he safe?'

'I don't see why he wouldn't be. I haven't heard any complaints.'

'Well, that's all right then.' Ouch. She can hear the sarcastic edge in her voice but she can't seem to do anything to prevent it. 'What's good enough for the locals is good enough for Susie. No point spending more on her than you think she's worth.'

Laura's standing just behind her. She says, 'Look, Andrea, I think I'll just go over to the cottage for a while. I've got some stuff to deal with.'

'Yes, of course.' She waits as Laura gathers up her things and walks carefully across to her own doorway. At the threshold she turns and waves. Andrea says, more gently, 'And did you see that girl Susie's got to help her? Was she there?'

'Alex? Yeah. She was fine. If you like that kind of thing. A bit of a waif. But Susie's good with strays. She always was.'

Andrea takes the little necklace out of its paper bag and runs it through her hand. 'If you could hear yourself when you talk about her . . . You sound very hard.'

'I was married to her. That's how you feel after it's over. It's all so easy when you're just setting out.'

She won't listen to him. He's just shooting his mouth off, as usual. Has he been drinking while she was gone? It's hard to be sure. Perhaps he and that taxi-driver guy went to the village bar together and had a couple of beers before Jim dropped him off? It seems more than likely. She says, 'Talking of journeys . . .'

'Which we weren't.' He stands up and moves towards the back door. She follows him. He opens the fridge and reaches for a bottle of dry Martini. She puts a restraining hand on his arm and he jerks her away angrily. 'Fuck off!'

She doesn't say anything else. She goes upstairs to their bedroom to shower and change. Jim's trousers are lying across the bed where he's thrown them and she picks them up and zips up the fly and hangs them in the wardrobe. As she folds them something falls out of the pocket. It's a photograph of the baby, opening her arms to the photographer and laughing. But she's so . . . And I . . . It makes you want to cry out and reach for her and hold her in your arms. She can't believe Susie suddenly felt generous enough to give him this. He must have stolen it from her when her back was turned.

As she closes the door she catches sight of herself in the mirror, a flash of light from the window, her hair damp with sweat and sticking to her cheeks. She's got shadows under her eyes. Her whole face looks slightly pinched. For a few seconds she can feel her mum's hands on her shoulders, hear her mum's voice saying, *Darling, what is it? Are you taking proper care of yourself?* She slips the little picture of Jade back into his pocket quickly, before she can change her mind.

A week later she still hasn't decided. She's phoned Will twice over the weekend, but he hasn't been able to tell her much. Their mother isn't any better, but she doesn't seem to be obviously any worse. She still can't manage to get out more than a few words. Her face still looks sort of droopy on one side. She can just about waggle the fingers on her left hand. When Andrea comes home from one of her private pupils to find Jim drinking beer with Jean-Marc and Louis, she loses patience and shouts at all three of them, a long tirade in such fluent French she can hardly believe it's come out of her own mouth. Jean-Marc grins up at her from under his fringe, his wiry, dark hair grey with cement-dust. Louis splays his fingers on the white plastic table, looking down at his broken nails.

She goes back into the kitchen and waits for them to leave, listening for them to walk past the window. At last the truck revs in the yard and drives away.

Then Jim's standing in the doorway. She's washing some raspberries her pupil's father gave her, the little red globules turning dark under the cold tap, oozing juice. Without looking up, she says, 'Why do you have to do this? You know we've got that thing at Pete and Liz's this evening. I don't want to get there at eight with you already half cut!'

He shifts his weight. 'One beer. That's all it was.'

'Okay.' She won't get at him, she won't say anything else. 'But I'm not driving.'

'I'll stay on the soft stuff. I don't mind.'

And he doesn't seem to. He's smiling at her, shaking his head, as if she's being childish. And perhaps I am. Perhaps it's all in my own imagination. Perhaps he doesn't really drink any more than anyone else our age. And perhaps, back home in Sussex, Mum's still her old self, wanting to hear all about our lives, making one of her Victoria sponges, or tramping to the top of Bott's Hill in the wind and rain on Boxing Day afternoon. If I cross my fingers and believe it perhaps it'll turn out to be the truth.

They're all here – not just Pete and Liz themselves, but their son, back for the summer from university somewhere in England, and his girlfriend, who turns out to be the girl Susie's got in to help her with the baby, and a few of the couples from the tennis club. That Chloë woman's here, with her classy husband. And Laura, of course. A few other odd bods Andrea hasn't met. And even the little lad from Les Platanes, with a stunningly pretty dark girl she hasn't seen before. She's vaguely aware of them hanging back on the periphery, his arm around her waist. And again later, playing table-tennis with Jack and Alex under the lights, the four of them leaping about and carrying on some sort of crazy conversation, screaming with laughter when the white ball glances off and plops into Laura's glass. There's something about all of them – a kind of animal energy that holds them all together. Perhaps it's sex: they're certainly the age for it. Or is it a kind of love? She looks over towards where Jim is. He's surrounded by people, talking as ever, his face lit up from underneath by the candles in their little glass pots. Does he even know how attractive he is? He's drinking something clear in a tall glass. Water? Lemonade? It could be either. There's nothing so far to suggest he isn't sticking to his word.

She picks up her own wineglass and edges nearer. He's in the middle of some long, complicated story. Around him his listeners seem completely absorbed, grinning with quiet amusement. Even Pete seems to have managed to shake off his usual moroseness. She sees him pick up what has to be a whisky and swill it in his mouth appreciatively before swallowing it down. What story can Jim possibly be telling? She hears Liz say, 'You must be very proud of her.'

'Oh, absolutely.' He leans forwards, fumbling in the pocket of his trousers. 'She's fantastic – if only my delightful wife would let me anywhere within three miles of her. Here. Have a look.'

She hears a nervous laugh. But they take the little photo and squint at it in the candlelight, passing it reverently from hand to hand. 'She's gorgeous,' Liz says. 'I *have* caught a glimpse of her occasionally, with Susie. But I hadn't realised just what a little sweetie she was.'

Behind her something rustles. It's Jack and Alex, both of them pale in the blue glow from the pool. They're holding hands. She sees them turn and move away into the shadows. After a while she hears a splash and looks round to see Jack's wet head bobbing like a seal's in the pale blue water. One by one the watchers stand up and throw off their clothes and go to join them in the pool. Jim hasn't even noticed her standing there. She picks up his glass and sniffs the contents. Hm. Mainly just melted ice: it's hard to be sure. She raises it to her lips. Lemonade. Is there a trace of vodka in there somewhere as well? In the pool someone's splashing and screaming. A drop of water hits the back of her hand. Jim's shirt and trousers are draped over the back of his chair. She feels for the little picture and slips it into the inside pocket of her handbag, pushing it gently right down to the bottom and closing the zip.

It takes so little . . . She lets herself curl in against the rough upholstery of the car seat, feeling the shadows move across her face, the dark shapes of trees. In front, the solid outline of Laura at the wheel. From the passenger side a pale strand of Alex's hair gleams in the lights from the house as they back away. When they get near Champfleury she'll have to be ready to give Laura directions to Susie's.

But not yet. She feels suddenly sleepy, her eyes begging to be allowed to close. When I was a child we'd drive home like this sometimes, Dad driving and Mum in the front at his elbow, talking to each other quietly while I lay stretched out full-length across the back seat. I'd watch the moon swim out abreast of the car, ducking in and out between the tops of trees. I was safe then. With them. And the roads were almost empty. Dad hardly ever had to dip his headlights. England then was like France now. Her eyes won't stay open any longer. Safe. Perhaps in spite of everything it's all going to be all right.

She feels her body relax against Jim's, her flesh juddering with the uneven surface of the road. He puts his arm round her shoulders and pulls her close to him, kissing the top of her head. She can't actually smell any alcohol on his breath. Perhaps he really is being straight with me. Mum always used to tell me my imagination was too vivid, that if I'd only see what was in front of my nose and nothing else, none of it would be so frightening or hurt so much.

Mum. As they climb the stairs to the bedroom she says, 'Jim, I've got to go back.'

He doesn't bother to put the light on. He comes over and stands behind her at the window, looking out with her at the gravelled yard. There's a three-quarter moon, and the uneven old roof-tiles stand out clear and distinct, separated by furrows of darkness. He says, 'I know.'

She twists to look at him. 'But . . .' His eyes are gleaming.

'Your Mum's had a stroke. I know. I spoke to Will on the

phone the other evening.'

'Then why . . . ?' It's crazy. He hasn't even mentioned it! What's wrong with him, for God's sake? She reaches to close the shutters and they swing slowly towards her, meeting with a small thud. She moves away from him and turns on the bedside lamp. She begins to undress slowly. Why hasn't he said anything? She crosses her arms and pulls her silk top up over her head, shaking her hair loose. 'And you didn't even think to mention it? Why on earth not? Did you think I'd freak out or something? Or have you decided my family's none of your business, is that it?'

'I wanted to leave you free.' He's undressing now too, turned away from her, the knobs of his spine showing under the skin as he reaches forward. 'I thought you should be free to make up your own mind.'

'How very delicate.' She winces as she says it. She's beginning to sound almost like him. But it's impossible to keep the sarcasm out of her voice.

He doesn't say anything. She feels him slide in under the sheet, their two bodies just touching. He's lying on his back with his elbows jutting on the pillow, his hands under his head. In spite of herself she's nuzzling against him, kissing the soft place at the side of his ribs, where the sun never reaches. 'You're such a funny man,' she says into his body. 'Do you ever stop and think about just how unusual you are?'

'Not often.' He unclasps his hands and turns towards her. His blue-grey eyes look darker in the lamplight, puzzled. He says, 'Would you like me to go back to England with you?'

'Oh, no.'

'You won't find it too much, on your own?'

'I won't be on my own.'

'You know what I mean.'

'Yes.' She suddenly sees herself as a girl of twelve – potato-flesh, short hair, the shapeless navy skirt and scratchy blazer. Her mum's tired face creased up with concern. *What do you mean, you can't face it? What's the matter with you?* She blinks and it's gone. 'Will'll be there. And my father. I'll be perfectly okay.'

'If you're sure.' He sounds doubtful.

'I am.' She reaches to turn off the lamp, waiting for her eyes to get used to the darkness. She isn't the slightest bit sleepy any more. The moonlight's not as bright as it was. Behind the shutters she sees a faint flicker of lightning.

'Well, I can drive you to the airport anyway, and see you off.'

'You don't even need to do that. It'd mess up a whole morning's work. I'll get that Damien guy from the village.'

He's starting to touch her. There really is no trace of alcohol on his breath or skin. I've been maligning him. And all she wants is to get closer, to melt into him somehow, be someone else on the way to somewhere else and never arrive. Not to have to leave him and go back to England and see my mum looking lopsided and pathetic, and be helpless to do anything about it, and have to pretend. Wanting to scream, *But this isn't you! You were never like this! Pull yourself together!* Feeling the eyes of the nurses as I unwrap the chocolates or the flowers. Desperate just to get back here to France, or turn back the clock. He says, into her neck, 'Well, I can come and meet you anyway, when you fly back.'

She feels him enter her. He lies still inside her for a moment, then starts moving slowly as her body expands in welcome. Meet me. Yes. Can't think about it now. But of course he'll be there waiting, when . . . He'll be here in

France, waiting at the barrier, miles away from all that. On one side of the Channel, something grey and formless and all-enveloping, something that doesn't bear thinking about; on the other side, work, friends, sunlight, mist rising like steam between the trees. She feels him moving inside her and the two countries seem to slide closer. Here every inch of her body is alive. He moves inside her and the two visions begin to blur and bleed. In some giddy air-shaft of the spirit she feels her own body falling and hears herself say, *death*. Her face aches with the effort of not coming, of making this last for ever, of never having to go back.

DAMIEN

The place was a shit-hole. He lay on the bed smoking, the smoke rising straight from his hand to the ceiling to spread itself in a blue fog. A thin shaft from between the shutters fell across the tangled bedclothes like a knife-blade across collapsed cheese. It stank. He stank. He changed the cigarette from his right hand to his left and sniffed at his fingers. They smelled of smoke; his body was smoked right to the bone. In the thin light from between the shutters even his nails showed yellow on the thumb and first two fingers of his right hand.

It was Christiane's fault. His own fucking sister. Why couldn't she clean the place up once in a while? That's what she did in those fucking English people's houses – she'd be out there every weekend, scrubbing and cleaning, and for what? So another load of pale-faced Brits with their fat, screaming kids could come and spread out their flabby, white bodies on sun-loungers at the side of a pool. And meanwhile she left him to live here in this pig-sty with dirty cups and glasses and socks and underwear all over the floor.

He stood up and went to the french windows, reaching between them to unlatch the shutters and fold them back. The sun was dazzling. It lit up the trees, the hydrangeas, the car parked in the lane outside. Through his screwed-up eyes the sky was a bleached slit. He stubbed the cigarette out in a nearby glass and started to rake about on the floor for his shirt and jeans. When he lifted the slipped covers from the floor he came across a woman's red satin thong, trimmed with lace. Josiane's. He raised it to his nose and breathed in. No smoke without fire! He found himself smiling as he remembered. Even if she did get up at some ungodly hour and drive back to town to that office job of hers, even if she did leave him here like a pig in shit, even if it was only the once a week she said she could manage and the rest of the time he was on his own.

Well, not always. He was grinning to himself again. There was Marika, over in Toulouse. There was Louise, though she'd let herself go a bit lately, she was fat, she didn't really turn him on that much – it wasn't the same as it had been when they first met. And that little red-haired girl he'd picked up that time a couple of years ago from the airport – she hadn't seemed all that keen initially but she'd had nowhere to spend the night and in the end she hadn't minded. And he kept his eyes open. There was always the chance of something. Women always seemed to find him pretty attractive, one way or another. He didn't have to make that much of an effort. And sometimes even the most unexpected situations could turn into something quite interesting and unusual – you never knew.

He pushed open the door to the passage, and then the heavier door to the kitchen, yawning. Christiane was chopping shallots on a board. A pile of tomatoes took up space at one end of the table, some of them as big as his hand. She looked up at him and frowned, wiping her eyes with the back of her wrist. 'You decided to get up, then?'

'Tu m'emmerdes.'

She turned back to her chopping without answering and he moved about the kitchen, pouring old coffee from the pot into a saucepan and putting it on to the stove to heat. He lit another cigarette and saw her purse her lips. He said, 'What's the matter? Don't you like your baby brother's nasty little habits? I'm so sorry. Let me take myself and my filthy cravings out of your good, right-thinking citizen's way.'

'Don't be so sensitive.'

'Oh, forget it.' He doused the cigarette with water from the dripping tap with a hiss and left it lying on the draining-board. He spat a shred of wet tobacco into the sink. 'One of these days I'll be out of here. And then you'll wish you could have me back – you'll miss having someone to get up your nose and keep you up to the mark. I'll leave an almighty hole in your life. You'll see.'

Christiane put the knife down and looked at him, her hands on her hips. The juice from the onions was pricking the inside of his nose. 'I don't really want to get rid of you. I just wish you wouldn't be so . . .'

He shrugged. 'I'm twenty-eight. What do you expect?'

'Bernard wasn't like that at twenty-eight.'

'Bernard's a clod.'

He could tell from the way she stood that he'd hurt her feelings. She'd picked up the knife again and was using it to scrape the little crumbs of shallot into a bowl. 'You wouldn't get far on your own without him.'

He hunched his shoulders, pushing his hands deep into his pockets. 'You think I don't earn enough to live on?'

'You don't.'

'I could.'

'Oh, yes. You *could*. If you worked proper hours. If you didn't spend half your life in bars or lying in bed.'

When he bothered to pull himself up straight he was easily taller than she was. He looked down at her thick, slightly greasy brown hair. The roots were darker, where she'd tried to use some sort of cheap colour to disguise the first few threads of grey. 'I sorted out that stupid Englishwoman's washing-machine.'

'Did she ask you to?'

'He did. The husband. We went over there together. I just rake around in her insides for a bit and she's all set up, good as new. I can do all sorts of shit. You don't know the half of it. Money for old rope. You should try it yourself. All you do is change a gas-bottle or rewire a plug and they can't thank you enough. She'll be round here begging me for it one of these days, you wait. Either her or the little girl who looks after the baby. I wouldn't say no to that one, I can tell you. Skinny, blond, arse like . . .' He uses his hands to sketch Alex's shape in the air.

Christiane said, 'Oh, grow up! You could make that taxi business pay if you put a bit more effort into it. You could even build up the handyman stuff on the side. And get some little place of your own where you wouldn't have me nagging you all the time. Get married even. I don't blame Josiane for getting fed up. I don't know how she stands it, I really don't.'

'What little place? There aren't any little places. The Brits have bought them all and converted them into fucking holiday lets. Have you seen the prices lately? They're astronomical. You've got to have made it these days even to shell out for some fucking two-room attic somewhere. We're talking real money.' He rubbed together the thumb and middle finger of his right hand. 'They all have their fat redundancy cheques, they all have mummies and daddies who pop off and leave them a few hundred thousand just when they happen to be thinking of getting their place in the sun. What chance is there for people like us?' The coffee was bubbling against the thin sides of the saucepan. He lifted it from the flame, reaching with his other hand to turn off the gas. The hot liquid spat at him as he poured it into a bowl. He carried it over to the table and sat down, raising it to his mouth with both hands.

She'd stopped working, her knife poised over the first of the tomatoes as she gazed past him at the open window. He turned to see what she was looking at and caught a blur of moving green and yellow, the lit speck of an insect flying past. She said, 'But you're not even trying. People are always telling me how offhand you are. The car's a disgrace. Half the time you don't even bother to answer the phone when it rings.'

He said easily, 'They'll find me if they want me.'

She gave a little laugh and went back to slicing the tomato, her serrated blade cutting the flesh into deft slivers. 'Are you sure?'

'They always seem to get me if they keep trying.'

'How do you know? They may just have given up. What about yesterday when you were in there snoring your head off and I answered? Some woman saying she needed a lift to the airport, and I said could I take a message, but she said no, she'd ring again. And of course she hasn't. It's not the first time.' She cut out the core of a tomato and pushed it to the side of the board with a small precise gesture.

He said, 'What woman?'

'The dark Englishwoman from up at Lermitte. The teacher.'

She meant Jim MacLaren's woman. Andrea. He shrugged. 'Did she say what day?'

Christiane sniffed. 'I've got a feeling she said Monday. But I wouldn't bank on it. You've lost that one. I'd be surprised if she ever bothered to ask you to take her anywhere again.'

'Relax. They know me. She'll keep trying. And besides . . .'

She was waiting for him to finish, her eyebrows raised, her forehead creased into a mass of little parallel wrinkles. 'Besides . . . ?' she prompted him.

'I'm going up that way this morning. I can call in, see if the guy's around. She's a beautiful woman,' he said. The words rang oddly even to his own ears.

He saw her immediately through the kitchen door, a shape moving backwards and forwards on the other side of the gauze curtain, undeniably female. He raised his fist and rapped against the glass and she lifted her head and came towards him. She stood for a moment in the open doorway, waiting for him to speak, and he was struck again by something in her expression, a slight lift of her eyebrows – was she looking down her nose at him? It wasn't the face women usually met him with. He leaned against the outside wall, pushing his hands down into his pockets. 'You wanted a car to take you to the airport on Monday, is that right?'

She didn't deny it. She'd rung someone else in the meantime, but it wasn't too hard to persuade her to cancel. He named a figure, regretting it instantly. It was far too low. How could he expect to make the business pay if he didn't even ask enough to cover his overheads? His sister was right. If he didn't look out he'd be trapped here for the rest of his life. And in this case it hadn't done him any favours. The stupid bitch was staring at him with something that looked almost like hostility. She said, 'You will be here when you say you will?' A lock of her dark hair hung down over the front of her T-shirt, curling just above where her breast started. He stopped himself from reaching out and coiling it round his finger.

She followed the direction of his eyes and turned away from him quickly, bending over the kitchen table to write something on a pad. She tore off the top sheet and handed it to him without a word. Like a fool he translated it back into English and read it back to her, tripping on the outlandish words. 'Be here Monday nine-thirty, arrive to the airport at eleven, okay? *C'est ça?*'

She nodded, barely glancing in his direction. She fancied the arse off him, obviously. He could have slapped her there and then, wiped that smile off her smug lips. And they'd have found themselves in bed together for the rest of the afternoon, that much was obvious. But he couldn't be bothered. So her wine-soaked rag of a husband couldn't get it up, poor frustrated cow. Well, that was her problem. Someone else might fall for that pathetic brand of English standoffishness, but not him. He'd got the measure of the British years ago, when he was only a kid, when that first crazy old couple had bought that derelict old barn over at Mirlac and paid him a few miserable francs to pick up the rotting apples in the autumn and sweep the leaves.

'Look,' Josiane said. 'Can we just go somewhere on our own for half an hour and talk?' She was dressing already, not even waiting for him to have his usual cigarette. She picked up his clothes from the floor and threw them at him. The shirt landed across his face and for a moment all he could see was blue.

He threw it off and sat up. 'Where do you suggest?'

'Somewhere where we can . . .' She gestured vaguely towards the door and he had a momentary vision of Christiane at the stove in her house-dress and slippers, Bernard slumped at the table, slurping soup on the other side.

'The Bar des Lilas?' he said. 'The Platanes? That's pretty quiet midweek. Why don't we go there?'

'Okay.' He heard her car keys clink as she closed her hand. 'I think I know where it is. But you go first and I'll follow you. You park down by the river, right?'

'Why don't we just take my car?'

But she had her determined face on, her jaw set in a line under her bobbed hair. 'I won't come back here afterwards. I'll just drive straight home from there.' She felt in her bag for a tissue and blew her nose. She didn't look that well – tired and older, the skin pouching slightly under her eyes, the line at the corner of her mouth sharper. She looked her age. But women were always worrying about one thing or another. For once he remembered to pick up her jacket and hold it open round her shoulders and she shook her hair free over the collar, glancing up at him in surprise.

The Platanes was almost empty, just one other couple at the front window, and the proprietor's son and his dumpy little girlfriend playing some sort of card game in a corner to while away the time between customers. No sign of old Maurisse, or Jeannine. Josiane hardly seemed even to see them, her head lowered as she made her way towards a dimly lit table at the back. He ordered a coffee with a brandy chaser. She had tea.

When it came she spent a long time playing with the tea-bag, dragging it through the hot water in little circles, using the spoon to squash it against the side of the cup. Finally she pulled it out by its string and dropped it in the saucer. 'I was going to tell you – I'm going away for a bit.' She looked up.

He took a sip of the coffee, then of the brandy. 'Right,' he said. 'Is it a holiday or what?'

She was looking at him over the rim of the cup. 'I thought I'd spend a couple of weeks with my cousin. I haven't seen her for ages.'

Her cousin. How boring was that? He leaned back in his chair, staring at the ceiling through the hanging smoke. He'd have to get on to Louise again, see what she was doing these days, whether she'd managed to smarten up her act and lose any weight since the last time. He said, 'When do you think you'll be back?'

'Oh . . .' She put down the cup and shook her head, her hair glinting under the light. She had nice hair. Nice breasts. Good hands and mouth.

For form's sake he said, 'Who is this cousin? Where does she live? You haven't mentioned her until now.' But he couldn't give a shit who she was. She could be the Queen of fucking England for all he cared. And good luck to her. There were plenty more where Josiane came from, two or three of them already waiting at the end of a phone.

'She's in Lyon, remember? We called in there once on our way back from the Jura. I just . . . I need to . . . I thought it would be a change.'

'Right.'

There didn't seem to be any more to say. He called the boy over and paid the bill. Josiane stood up to put her jacket on.

She looked up briefly as she was doing up the buttons and gave him an odd little smile. Well, he wasn't going to get into that stupid mind-reading stuff women were always so keen on. Let her smirk if she wanted to, he wasn't going to rise to it. She could keep her fucking thoughts to herself. It didn't make an atom of difference, all that 'tell me your deepest feelings' shit, it didn't sharpen up her performance one little bit.

Outside, the evening air was cool on his skin. In the darkness under the plane-trees he pulled her to him and kissed her, running his tongue along the inside edge of her lips until her mouth opened. After a while she put her hand flat on his chest and pushed him gently away.

He was far too early. Nine-thirty, she'd said, and the clock on the dashboard read 8.15. She'd got to him, the stupid bitch, she'd made him nervous. And now here he was like a schoolboy, waking up too soon for some pathetic test or other and finding he'd got time to kill, running round in circles just to pretend he didn't give a fuck. But anything was better than sitting at the kitchen table listening to Christiane go on about how he ought to pull his finger out, blah blah, how he really ought to try a bit harder, so he could have the pleasure of sleeping in some little attic cupboard somewhere and forking out three times the proper rent. Let her move out if she wanted to. And that lump of a husband of hers. Let them both rot in their own pathetic little lives.

He drove to the top of the village and parked in a crook of the lane next to the MacLaren woman's place to smoke a cigarette. He wound down the window and spat a loose shred of tobacco into the weeds at the side of the road. Then he inhaled. That was better. The sharp smoke seemed to touch something into life deep inside his brain. Around him the village was turning over, stretching in the sun. Somewhere over his shoulder a cock crowed. To his left he caught the hiss and glitter of water – old ma Pirottet watering her plants with a hose. Above him in the converted farm-buildings a shutter grated open and he saw the little blond English girl lean out, her long pale hair brushing the sill. So that was where her bedroom was. He could sit here for quarter of an hour, almost out of sight, and he might find out something useful – whether the boyfriend slept there with her, for instance. Whether she looked like a cat that's been at the cream, or whether there might be something a bit wistful about her to tell him he was in with a chance. She looked down and their eyes met briefly. She drew her head in and closed the window. He took another drag from the cigarette and let his wrist hang limp outside the car, watching the smoke curl up between his fingers into the still air.

As he drove through the village he had the odd sense that something had changed. Something white slid across his rear-view mirror as he passed the playground, too quickly for him to see what it was. He turned the car at the grass triangle and drove back.

The door of the pilgrims' shelter was hanging open. He pulled it wider and looked inside. There was litter on the floor – a greasy-looking twist of paper, an empty cigarette-packet. He shoved them into a corner with his foot. He closed the door, blinking in the sunlight. There was a smell too – something sharp and vaguely sweet – had someone been using the place to pee or smoke in? Outside on the grass, one of the swings hung at an angle, its rope twisted into a knot. He unravelled it and turned the tyre seat over, picking away a lump of chewing-gum that had hardened on the rim. He sat down and pushed away with his feet, doubling his long legs under so they didn't scrape against the scar of bare earth underneath, the horizon rising and falling hypnotically with the movement of his eyes. Good for them, he found himself thinking. Let them all come and pump their bodies full of drugs and leave the place like a pigsty and piss in the corners and break the door down. It was an eyesore anyway, it was a joke, no one in their right mind would even consider walking all that way like some down-and-out, nothing better to do than start in Arles and hobble all the way west and south as far as the Spanish border and beyond, pissing and puking and shitting on everything as they went.

He grinned, thinking of the places, all the towns and villages strung between here and Toulouse like beads on a string – Léguevin, Giscaro, Auch, Montesquiou, Aubrillac – he'd driven through them all. They were all mindless, comatose even, smug as a pig in shit, they'd all got it coming. In his mind's eye they merged to a single small-town square with a crumbling stone arcade and plane-trees and benches where old men sat and watched each other tossing boules into the dirt. The walkers were welcome to it, or the Brits, whoever. None of it was worth quarrelling over, there was nothing worth getting excited about or cleaning or preserving. The small working farms of his childhood had gone, and the people with them, fused by some invisible napalm into a single monstrous body that no one recognised or cared about keeping alive. No wonder the English had had such an easy time of it. The whole place had been waiting, just crying out for them to come and swarm all over it in their Land Rovers, like the Germans had in their tanks sixty-odd years ago, before he was born.

The swing had swayed to a stop. He heard a noise some-where over to his left and looked up. But it was only a bird – a magpie, pecking at a shred of sausage-rind left by the walkers. He stood up, reaching into his pocket again for his cigarettes and lighter, and it clattered off, flapping its black wings. He had a sudden clear picture of Josiane swinging her black leather jacket across her narrow shoulders. What was it she'd said to him? Had she actually told him it was a holiday? You stupid . . . He almost hit himself on the forehead. Of course! She was going to spend some time in the city so she could look for a job. She was leaving him. She'd had enough. She wasn't coming back. And all he'd be left with was Louise – fucking Louise with her wonky lipstick and cellulite thighs – that was what he'd got to look forward to – unless he could manage to get there and make Josiane see sense in time.

From the church down by the main road he heard the clock strike nine. God! Was that how late it was? He'd got to go. The Englishwoman up at Lermitte – Andrea, was that her name? – was expecting him to be there at half past to take her to the fucking airport. What the hell could he have been thinking about, to fall for something so fucking stupid? Hadn't he got enough to think about? But it was okay, it had to be. No one could move quite that fast. He'd take the woman and then, as soon as he got back, he'd drive over to Tarbes and find Josiane and talk her through it all sensibly. And she'd change her mind, she always did. He knew where she worked. All he had to do was just drive there and find out where she'd parked her car and pull in next to it and sit and wait.

DAMIEN

He switched on the engine and started to drive away. But something was wrong. The steering felt squishy and unresponsive under his fingers. And through the open window came a loud noise – a sort of flapping. Everything seemed to be at an odd angle, his seat tipping him slightly sideways, as if the car was sinking at one corner. The sound he could hear was partly the loose tyre flapping as it turned, partly the metal wheel-rim grating across the gravel of the verge.

Shit! It was all he needed. He stopped the car and got out to have a look. It was as he expected: the nearside tyre was completely flat. Those fucking pilgrims – there was a rock left lying at the edge of the road, and he hadn't seen it, he'd been so preoccupied he'd driven straight over. And now look. The tyre was completely ripped, hanging off and trailing like a rag of blackened skin. And they didn't give a fuck. All they did was just walk through, leaving their mess behind, and this was the result. He'd like to watch one of them stumble over a rock and fall flat on his face in the path and see how he reacted.

He got back in and reversed slowly to the place he'd just left. At least he'd got his tool-kit in the boot. And thank God he'd finally thought to replace that spare tyre after what happened last time. That was – what? – only a few months ago. They said lightning never struck in the same place twice, but he must be the exception. Trust him to be unlucky. He seemed to spend half his time changing wheels these days.

He felt for the rusty jack and reached in under the car to position it next to the wheel. Somewhere behind him the clock struck the hour and he found himself counting the strokes. Only just nine. If he was quick he could still just about make it – maybe a few minutes late, but still plenty of time to get to the airport by eleven, if the stupid bitch only had the sense to sit tight and not get herself all worked up. All she had to do was wait. He bent to loosen the wheel-nuts, then stood up and started to pump the jack with his foot and the heavy old Citroën began to lift slowly, raising itself breath by breath from its sideways slump of defeat.

He knelt down to the wheel, swearing as one of the nuts resisted him and the spanner flew out of his grip, landing with a clatter halfway across the road. He stood up and went over to pick it up. The sweat was running down the inside of his shirt. He'd got grease on his hands. Should he give the woman a quick call on his mobile to let her know he'd been held up, that he was on his way? But he wasn't sure he'd taken her number. And if he had it might only make her panic and try and get someone else. And it would make him even later. Better to just get on with it, it wasn't really taking all that long. He had the odd feeling that time was standing still. Hadn't the village clock struck the same hour twice, as it always did? In a few minutes it would strike again, and it would be nine o'clock for a third time. And then a fourth and a fifth. By the time the spare tyre was in place and he was ready to slide himself into the driving-seat and restart the engine it still couldn't be much after nine. Between the jumbled roofs of the village the cocks were still crowing; old ma Pirottet was still on the other side of the hedge in her flowered overall and slippers, waving a hose over her dripping plants. And he was just passing through, on his way up to Lermitte to pick up Jim's woman and take her to the airport. Nothing had happened. No blow-out, no wrestling-match with the wheel-nuts – he'd dreamed up the whole thing. All he had to do now was drive down the lane past the playground and up to where she lived. The car felt fine, the steering-wheel firm and responsive under his fingers, all four of his tyres intact.

As he was kneeling to pack up his tools, he heard someone turn on their ignition on the other side of the stone arch. He straightened up and stood waiting, the oily bundle still in his hand. As Susie came through the gate she slowed and leaned out of the window to speak to him in French. 'Are you okay? Is anything the matter?'

He shrugged. 'It's done.'

She was looking at him from behind her sunglasses, taking the situation in. 'Well, do go in and wash your hands if you feel like it. I've got to go out, but Alex is there. She'll look after you.'

'Thanks.' He watched her car disappear down the lane, towards the triangle. He looked down at his hands. They were filthy, nails full of muck, the lines across his palms drawn in black. She was quite right – he couldn't go and pick someone up in that state. Much better to spend just a moment scrubbing himself off. And how long could it possibly take anyway? Five minutes at most. What were five minutes? He'd give her a call on the mobile. He leaned into the car to open the glove-compartment, but even before he felt inside he had a vision of his handset, lying next to his dirty bowl on the yellow and blue flowered oilcloth of the kitchen table. Well, there was nothing he could do about it now. And five minutes wouldn't make any difference either way. If she couldn't wait five minutes she wasn't worth worrying about. It would still be only just after nine by the time he set out.

At first he couldn't make the girl hear. He opened the door a crack and poked his head in. The baby was there, strapped into her chair, craning backwards to look at him, but there was no sign of anyone else. Then he caught a movement at the window. She was out there in the garden, pegging little clothes on to a line stretched between two old apple trees. He edged towards the sink. She still hadn't seen him. He turned on the tap and waited for the water to run hot. He reached for the washing-up liquid and squirted a thin stream over his hands.

When she saw him she almost screamed. 'What are you . . . ?' She was standing in the opening with the green and gold of the garden at her back, her hair lit up round her head with sun, the empty laundry basket in her arms.

'Sorry.' He could feel himself grinning sheepishly as he told her about the tyre and about Susie driving past. After a while the girl seemed to relax, putting the basket down and leaning back against a cupboard, her bare legs crossed one over the other, her weight on one espadrilled foot. When she next spoke it was to offer him a cup of coffee.

He thought about it. He'd lost a bit of time already and he was due up at Jim's place at – what? – nine-forty-five? But the odd minute or two couldn't make any difference one way or the other. Everyone knew the check-in times at airports these days were completely unrealistic. You could get there half an hour before the plane was due to take off and still find yourself twiddling your thumbs for ages while they farted about with God knows what. And if you got there when they said, you were kicking yourself. He watched the little shadow at the girl's wrist flicker in and out as she set the glass jug on the table, measured the coffee into it and poured the hot water. A snake of her pale hair threatened to slide over the lip of the jug and she caught it just in time, hooking it firmly behind her ear. The steam was making her pink. Over by the window, the baby bounced in her chair and then went quiet, chewing on the head of a plastic animal. Was it supposed to be a sheep? The girl glanced over in the baby's direction and smiled. After a while she pushed down the plunger and filled two small cups, adding a splash of milk to her own. He took a sugar lump from the box she offered him and held it just above the surface, watching the brown tidemark rise through the grains slowly until it reached his finger and thumb and he was forced to let go. 'So . . . *are you enjoying here?*' he said.

She was sitting opposite him now. She opened her eyes wide at his question and he saw they were a very pale blue-grey. She was watching him over the rim of her cup. She answered him in French. 'Not bad.' Her eyes wandered to a point somewhere over his left shoulder. 'It feels like a long time since I came.'

'I picked you up at the station,' he said. 'That first day.'

'Yes.' She was smiling as she groped for the words. 'You drove me here. And Susie showed me the flat. It was shut for a week. It was very hot.'

Should he risk it? She was so young and sweet. He said in English, 'Your French has made many progress since. You know, you could start to speak very well if only you had someone French to practise.'

She was frowning. Shit. He tried again. 'We could drive up to Mirlac, swim in the lake, have a meal in the Truite d'Or one evening. And talk. That's what language are for. To talk to someone.'

She pushed her chair back and went over to where the baby was still playing under the window. The plastic sheep had rolled on to the floor and Jade was reaching for her own toes, each little pink foot haloed in sunlight. Alex crouched in front of her and took her hands and clapped them together until he heard a squeal of laughter. In a moment she was standing in front of him with the baby in her arms, the little fingers grasping at a strand of her hair. She stood there, shifting her weight from one foot to the other, rubbing her cheek against the baby's soft head. He understood suddenly that she was waiting for him to leave. 'Well, thanks.' He pushed back his own chair and moved backwards towards the door. 'I'd better go. I've got to take someone to the airport.' He took a step backwards, feeling for the handle of the door behind him. 'Would you mind if I just used your phone?'

'Go ahead.' She gestured to where it stood, on one of the kitchen cupboards. He pulled out his little notebook and started to dial the number self-consciously, his fingers slipping on the keys. He cursed under his breath and started again. Alex moved away discreetly into the garden, leaving him to hold his conversation in private.

He punched the numbers in slowly one by one, intent on not making another mistake. But when he put the receiver to his ear all he heard was the long ringing tone, going on and on. The silence at the other end was thick and heavy; you could almost feel it. No one was going to answer. He knew anyway, he could tell from the sound of his own breathing in the receiver that she'd already gone. There was no one at the end even to pick up the phone and shout at him angrily to pull his finger out and make sure he bloody well got there soon.

So she'd decided to give up on him. She'd rung someone else – that other guy she'd mentioned in Ferdier – and he'd taken her. Or she'd called her husband on his mobile and he'd rushed back from wherever he was and driven her to the airport in his car. It was no big deal. They had money, these people. Things were easy. She'd probably even had time to strip off and have a quick dip in the pool just before she left.

Bitch. He found himself smiling as he remembered the smooth, brown skin of her arms and neck, the way her breast swelled gently under her T-shirt, how he'd been close enough to reach out and touch her, feel the soft shape of her resting in his hand. Well, she'd be back. And if she wasn't there were plenty more. If all else failed there was Marika, or Louise. Or even . . . He looked up. Alex had come back in from the garden, the little pig of a baby still in her arms. Listening for him to finish, obviously. He weighed her up – face, breasts, belly, hips, thighs . . . She wasn't that attractive really. It was all a bit limp and colourless and, well, English. He wasn't really sure he'd be all that tempted, even if she were begging for it, even if her hands were tied together and her feet and she were wearing just some sort of dark loin-cloth, her cheek swollen purple with bruises as he spat on her naked body, kicking her in the ribs while she sobbed and writhed under him in the dirt.

It took him longer than he'd expected to drive into Tarbes. Several kilometres before the ring-road he got stuck behind a tractor loaded with bales of straw, the yellow needles blowing back at him, surrounding his car as he drove. The dust was blowing in at the windows, getting in his throat, making his eyes itch until he had to take his hands off the wheel to rub them. For a while he had to drive with the glass rolled up and the heat was almost unbearable. He was suffocating. Then finally there was a straight stretch and he managed to rev up and overtake, drawing in just in time before a stream of oncoming cars swept past him in a rush of noise. The first driver blew his horn as he went by, a long blast. Fuck off, arsehole. How would he bloody like to be stuck behind that fucking thing kilometre after kilometre? You try it, mate. Be my guest. See how you feel when your throat's turned into sandpaper and you're nearly passing out for lack of air. He turned on the radio and a blast of music came out, so loud it made the old speakers rattle. But he was calming down, start-ing to hum along. It was something he recognised. After the first few bars he joined in, it was easy, he was cool, he could speak English almost like a native – *Feel her body rise. Will you kiss her mouth?* Wasn't this his own relaxed, inviting French voice singing the English words?

He reached the ring-road roundabout and took the town centre exit. Josiane's office was in one of the prefab blocks on the south side: it was quicker to cut straight across. But then he got snarled up on a corner where a truck was trying interminably to reverse into a narrow street. And meanwhile everyone else had to just sit at their wheels like imbeciles. Fortunately he had the radio. These places were never designed for those monsters, what the fuck did they have to let them in for. But it was the same everywhere you went. That was what it was like in this fucking country now.

He looked for her car in the staff car-park, but he couldn't see it. Was she off sick, then? Had she rung in to say she had a migraine? Surely she couldn't have come and gone already? He just wasn't looking properly. He nosed slowly up and down between the rows of parked cars, but it was no good. Her little red Renault definitely wasn't there. The sun bounced off the grey and white and silver bodies, making his eyes hurt; the gravelled surface under his wheels was white with dust. He stopped the car for a moment and leaned forward, resting his forehead on the wheel.

Perhaps she was just being clever. She'd had the presence of mind to park somewhere else because she'd known he'd come looking. On some quiet side-street not too far away from here her car would be sitting quietly at the kerb, its windscreen shielded from the inside by the old blanket she used to keep off the glare. All he had to do was ring her work number and she'd answer it with her sexy, slightly husky voice.

He drove around till he found a public phone. It was a mixed area, part offices, part industrial, with a few small newer developments of private houses. He rummaged in the side pocket for an old phone-card he'd had to buy once, ages ago, and rang the firm's number and her extension but again there was no answer – not even a ring-tone. He replaced the receiver, yanking at the card so fiercely it slipped from his fingers and fell to the floor of the booth. His scalp prickled with sweat. A drop ran down into his eye and he pushed it away with the back of his hand. He propped the glass door of the cabin open with his foot while he scrabbled for the card, then stood up and aligned it with the slot for a second time.

He tried again, dialling the company's general enquiry number. The girl on the switchboard told him the extension he wanted was temporarily unavailable and asked him if anyone else could help him with his problem. She said the words like some kind of fucking robot. 'Josiane Aubert,' he'd heard himself saying. 'Just give me Josiane.' In the end he was almost shouting it at her, he could hear his voice shaking. His hand was clenched on the receiver, the salt sweat stinging his eyes. He kicked the door open again and held it ajar with his foot while he tried to get some sense out of her. She was a cretin. For a long moment the line went dead. And then he was through to another woman, older, someone with a cut-glass northern accent who was obviously trying to make him feel about that high.

'I'm afraid no one of that name works here any more.'

'Yeah, she does. In invoices. The big room on the second floor at the end.'

'Madame Aubert has recently left the company.'

'She can't have. She was there yesterday, for fuck's sake.'

There was a short silence at the other end of the line. Then the voice said again, 'Madame Aubert is no longer with us.'

His mind went suddenly blank. It was like being about twelve again, turning a street corner and walking slap-bang into some arsehole of a teacher just when you were trying to light a cigarette inside the flap of your coat. What could he say? The stupid cunt was waiting for him to answer. He said, 'But didn't she have to give notice?'

The voice said, 'I'm not at liberty to discuss Mme Aubert's personal situation.' Then added, as if it were actually half-human, 'There's no reason to suspect any irregularity.'

He felt dizzy. He hung his head out of the box, stretching the flex of the phone as far as it would go. After a moment the feeling passed. From the receiver he could hear the woman's little voice squawking something and he raised it to his ear again. 'Are you still there?'

He grunted. 'I guess I can wait till she gets back and contact her at home.'

The woman said doubtfully, 'You can try.'

Was she telling him that Josiane had actually moved? He whistled inwardly. The devious fucking slut! He wouldn't have thought she had it in her. He heard his own voice say, 'Could you let me have her new address?'

'I'm afraid we can't do that.'

'Why the fuck not?'

There was a silence at the other end. She started to say, 'I don't—'

'Oh, forget it.' He went to hang up.

'We can forward something, if you'd like to send it care of the company. We'll make sure it reaches her.'

He had an urge to throw the receiver at the glass wall of the cabin. He leaned sideways to rest his weight against the glass but the heat of it made him snatch his hand away and rub his fingers across his thigh. 'Thank you,' he said. 'You've been most helpful. I'll send her a fucking bouquet.'

As he drove, he played the conversation over in his mind again. The low-roofed factories and warehouses gave way to flat fields of corn and sunflowers, and then to hills and green.

Sometimes he'd drive through a wood and sudden cool flowed in at the windows. Stupid arsehole of a woman he'd spoken to, it wasn't as if he even knew her. What did it matter what she thought of him? She'd probably been quite taken with his voice, if the truth were known. He heard himself again, his directness, the virile way he hadn't allowed her to have the last word. He remembered how her own official language had softened slightly in response.

And he could still find Josiane and bring her back. She'd said she was going to her cousin's in Lyon. And hadn't he been there with her once, didn't he have a pretty good idea of where she lived? It wouldn't take much just to drive there and find her. He saw himself ordering a drink at the bar of some little neighbourhood café, leaning forward to ask the proprietor a question. The man actually came to the door with him and pointed to a building a few doors up the street, his shiny face cracked open on a smile.

He was on the motorway now, speeding along at a hundred and thirty, a hundred and forty, a hundred and fifty even, the old car rattling and roaring under him with the pleasure of the open road. He overtook a new Peugeot, a convoy of trucks. The traffic was much lighter now. The sun was low on the horizon and the landscape had lost its sharp edges. He had both the front windows wide open and the cool air flowed over his face and arms. He pushed his spine hard into the seat-back and took a deep breath. So Josiane had left and now he was finally leaving as well. She was courageous. She'd seen that it was necessary and she'd taken her future in her own two hands. And who could blame her? There was that bad marriage she'd never quite got over, and now she was

getting older, she was beginning to look her age suddenly –
men weren't going to go on being attracted to her for ever.
And for her the clock was ticking: soon it would be too late
for her to have kids. You had to try and see it all through her
eyes. For her this could be the start of a whole new life.

Kids. He raised his hand from the wheel and ran it over
the lower part of his face. Could she possibly be . . . ? But
wouldn't she have . . . ? He saw her again in his mind's eye,
leaning forward over the café table, her dark jacket slung over
the back of the chair. What was it she'd said? 'I'm going
away for a bit.' It wasn't much to go on. 'I just . . . I thought
it would be a change.' Most of the oncoming cars had their
headlights on now. He flicked the switch and saw the dashboard controls leap into life.

If she'd made the break, he could do it too. He could leave
that whole fucking set-up – Bernard in his stinking overalls,
slumped in front of the TV in the kitchen, and Christiane
washing up interminably, the clapped-out old taxi and the
odd jobs – he could do something completely different. He
was good with his hands, and not stupid. There were all kinds
of things he could do. He could live with Josiane while he
took his time to look around. They could even get married
if that was what she wanted. He had a sudden picture of
the crown of her head, bent over a wedding catalogue, her
glossy hair hanging down, and he felt himself smiling. When
he found her he'd put his arms round her and pull her to
him and give her the longest, deepest kiss she'd ever known.
And he'd ask her to marry him – no real fuss, just the civil
ceremony in the Mairie, with her cousin and the proprietor
of the local café as witnesses. And if it turned out that she
really did want kids he'd agree to give the whole thing a bit

of thought, once they got on their feet.

His bladder was bursting. He stopped at a rest-area to relieve himself and stood by the car to light a cigarette, his mind churning. He could . . . They could . . . His hand was shaking on the wheel of the lighter and he could hardly get the tip of the cigarette to meet the flame. That was better. He took a second deep drag, shifting his weight and looking up at the poplar tree above him. It was dark now and the leaves shimmered, waving in the light of the electric lamp, sending little moving flakes of shadow over the ground at his feet. But . . . Something at the back of his mind still niggled. He heard the cold voice of the woman in Invoices. What was it she'd said to him? 'There's no reason to suspect any irregularity'? What the fuck was that supposed to mean?

He knew what it meant. It meant Josiane had been planning to leave for at least a month and hadn't bothered to drop him even so much as a hint of what was on her mind. It meant that wherever she was going, she was going without him – that he was part of what she was running from. Perhaps he was even the most important part. Wherever she was, she didn't want him there with her. He screwed up his eyes and massaged his forehead with his spread hand.

He got back in the car and drove on for a few kilometres. Lyon 36, the sign said. He was almost there. He settled back into his seat, grimacing. How fucking dense was it possible to be? What more did she need to do to you to make you understand? The old car rattled louder than ever. It sounded tired to him now. He slowed down to take the first exit slip-road and crossed over to the other side.

ANDREA

I t's just coming up to nine-thirty. She goes round the house, closing the shutters against the sun. Only the kitchen's cool enough to leave open, shaded by the big leaves of the fig-tree that grows against a corner of the old wall. She reaches into the fridge for a bottle of water. That's what she needs. The glass is slippery with condensation under her hand. Relax. She stands for a moment with her back against the edge of the sink and closes her eyes.

Fragments of French and English are still playing over in her head, the different voices interweaving. She can almost see the words, like an illuminated message travelling across a dark screen. But it's too urgent, and moving too fast. She barely has time to recognise a few letters before it's snatched away.

Stop it! She gives her head a little shake, as if she's got water in her ears. Don't think about any of them. Let them take care of themselves for once. Most of her students are on holiday anyway now. Just a few of the adult learners still around, still wanting their usual fix of English grammar and conversation, their weekly excuse to tell her haltingly about their lives and fill her hands with melons and apricots and pots of home-made jam. And it isn't as if she has any real alternative. One way or another, this is what she'll always be doing. She sees herself sitting with Régine, one of her more elderly students, encouraging her with every tiny muscle of her face and body in the hopeless search for a lost word. It's not really any different from encouraging someone who's lost their own language. A few hours and I'll be doing this in England. Only this time I won't feel as if I'm doing anything useful. This time the old woman will be my mum.

But she's got to do it. What kind of daughter would hear of her mother's illness and not come running? How can she even really think of staying away? She sees herself walking in through the heavy doors of the nursing-home and looking down at a pink and mauve flower-arrangement that can only have been salvaged from a recent funeral. She waits to be shown the way. *Mum? In this place?* She wants to turn on her heels and run. But she lets herself follow the nurse into the big day-room where her mum's a little old woman among the others, in a cardigan she hasn't seen before, with a plastic beaker of tea on a tray. Her dad's there, sitting on a chair in front of her with his hands between his knees. As she watches he leans forward to lift the beaker to her mum's lips. He mops her mouth with a cloth and looks across in Andrea's direction. She forces herself to step forward and kiss them both.

And her mum still is her mum. It's like the dreams she has of finding herself at the mouth of a deep hole, a sort of mine-shaft with impossibly steep sides and ragged, crumbling edges where all the people she's ever known are standing waiting for her to jump off. A rush of air and noise, and someone's body lying crumpled at the bottom – her mother's or her own. Which is it? She has to go to that edge and look over. If she can't bring herself to do this now she'll still be having nightmares about it for the rest of her life. But however coolly she tries to think about it she can still feel herself being drawn towards the edge of something, some kind of sick fall where her stomach flips over into emptiness with a gasp.

She pours herself another half-glass of water and puts the bottle back in the fridge. She's got to stop thinking. Damien will be here in a minute and then she'll be on the conveyor belt, all she'll have to do is sit there and in a few hours she'll be at her mother's side, without ever really being aware of having left.

But he's late. She looks at her watch. Nine-thirty-seven already. Somehow she's been assuming he'd be dead on time, that already he'd have lifted her small holdall into his boot and they'd be through Champfleury and well on their way. Where can he have got to? Her ears strain to catch the noise of his tyres on the gravel as he turns in, but all she can hear are wood-pigeons, a dog barking somewhere in the distance. Thank goodness she had the foresight to build in a bit of slack.

Nine-forty. It's twenty to nine in England. The breakfast trays will be gathered up by now, the spoons and bowls and bibs, the plastic beakers with their little spouts. It'll be time for the hoisting and toileting, the washing and patting dry and rolling over, time to change sheets and plump up pillows, to fish for dentures in their overnight glass. And Mum . . . What are they doing to Mum? No one's really told her whether her mum's only a bit slower and sadder than usual or whether she's turned into some terrifying other person with slurred speech and a face that sags on one side, someone who's going to blink at her own daughter without recognising her or remembering her name.

Well, Andrea will have to remember for both of them.

Hasn't she had a taste of it already, rescuing the big old photo-album last time she was in England and bringing it back here with her to France? Fingering the pictures of her and Will when they were little kids together, running some stupid race one hot August afternoon, their bare legs covered in scratches – Will's red T-shirt only just ahead of her, even though he was a year older, her dad bellowing encouragement from the side. And then she was falling, crashing to the ground, dry grass-stalks rasping her cheek, howling, *Mum! He tripped me, Will tripped me!* Her mother's almost imperceptible jerk of impatience as she knelt next to her with a crumpled tissue to wipe the tears away.

It's almost ten and there's still no sign. She lifts the receiver out of its cradle and dials his number. She can hear it ringing. She goes round to the front and stands watching the road with the phone still clutched against her ear. Then his sister answers, slightly breathless. He's already left.

'Was it a long time ago?' Since she's been there waiting the shadow of the old walnut-tree seems to have moved across the gravel a couple of inches.

'A good hour at least.' Christiane's voice falls sharply at the end of the sentence, as if to brook no argument. And there's something else, anxiety or exasperation, it's hard to be certain which.

'Has he got a mobile number I can ring?'

'He has, but he doesn't always remember to charge the battery. I'll give it to you anyway, and you can try.'

'Thanks.' But when she rings there's only the usual voice-mail message. The time's slipping away faster than she can track him down. It's almost ten past. Her hand's shaking as she puts in Jim's number and clutches the receiver to her ear. No answer there either. Where is he? She leaves a quick message and slips the receiver back into her pocket. The road's still empty, as far as the bend.

'Andrea?' It's Laura's voice, slow and sleepy-sounding, from somewhere over to her left. 'Is everything okay?' She's on one of the Adirondack chairs by the pool, in shorts and swimsuit, a big hat flopping over her sunglasses. 'I thought you were leaving at nine-thirty?'

'I was.'

'What happened? Didn't your cab come?'

'Not yet.'

Laura squints over the sunglasses at the watch on her brown wrist. 'It's nine fifty-five already.'

'I know.'

For a moment Laura sits there looking up at her, the book she was reading still open in her lap. Then she swings her legs to the paving-stones and pushes herself up. 'Come on. I'll give you a ride.'

'Are you sure?'

But Laura's already in the hall, picking up the bag. Already she's striding towards the hired car, her keys jingling from one finger. 'Are you serious? If you're not there in an hour you're not gonna make your flight.'

The sun's high already, bouncing off the metallic paint of the bonnet and making her screw up her eyes. She feels in her bag for her sunglasses and puts them on. They're smeared with fingerprints and she takes them off again and tries to rub them clean on the side of her skirt. The right-hand lens has got a deep scratch across it. If she closes her left eye the whole landscape's a blur. Ahead of them the surface of the road shimmers. She sees someone looming towards them — a couple standing on the grass verge. But no, it's only one of those life-size cut-outs, made of flat board and painted black. *So many injured, so many dead in so many years.* A moment, and they're past and shrinking in the wing-mirror. Laura closes the windows and turns on the air-conditioning. A field of sunflowers flies past them, the yellow faces all pointing the same way.

'Are you okay?' Laura glances at her sideways.

'Not really.' She has a sudden thought and rummages in her bag for her passport, then sits back in her seat. 'It's my own fault. I shouldn't have expected him to be reliable. He's French.' She hears herself saying it and winces.

'He's a man,' Laura says.

In her lap her hands are slick with sweat. She says, 'Not all men are wasters. Look at Jim. He hasn't got a mean bone in his body.'

'So you keep telling me.' They're closing on a lorry that's belching out dark fumes. She wills Laura to overtake, but she's hanging back, as if they've got all the time in the world. From behind them a small car draws out, trapping them in the truck's wake. It struggles abreast and stays there, its indicator still flashing. Laura's fingers lift on the steering-wheel and then relax. 'Wasn't he mean to Susie?' she says.

'Oh, well, Susie . . . Susie's his wife. Susie's a special case.'

'We're all special cases. If that's how he is with her what makes you so sure he'll be different with you?'

She forces herself to keep looking at the road ahead. People drive so fast here, and they're always right on your tail, just waiting to whizz past you at the first possible opportunity, the first straight stretch, and there are all these hills and hidden dips. It's so dangerous. Laura really has no idea. 'I don't know,' she says finally. 'I suppose I'm just hoping he will.'

Laura glances in her rearview mirror and slows slightly. A silver BMW sweeps past. 'You won't have to think about the cans and bottles he throws out while you're away anyhow. I'll make sure he stays on track.'

She wants to say, 'Don't bother.' She wants to say, 'That won't be necessary.' But can she be that sure of him? The sun hits the metallic blue paint of the bonnet in a hard star, making her eyes water.

'I wish you wouldn't worry about him,' Laura says. She's turned her head slightly sideways, half-looking in Andrea's direction: she's gone into counselling mode. 'This trip's for your mom. She needs you. You have to start thinking of this as her time.'

The flood plain's narrower now. They pass a steep field of dried mud and scrubby grass, dotted with enormous black birds. She feels the pressure of something hot and sour rising in her chest. She says, 'It's been her time for years – all the time we were growing up. It's my time now. It really is. I've only just begun.'

She's suddenly aware of the hum of the car engine. Laura leans forwards and twists something on the dashboard and the jet of cool air over her face and arms gets fiercer. It's hard to hear anything over the hiss of the fan. 'You know . . .' Laura's choosing her words carefully. 'It may not have been her fault. She may have been doing the best she could in her situation. Kids often don't understand what's happening with their parents. Have you ever asked yourself what things were actually like between them.'

It takes her breath away. How can Laura sit there and pass

judgement, as if she actually knows them, as if she has more insight than Andrea does herself? It's not even worth trying to answer. She turns her body slightly towards the window. Outside under a white sky something dry and yellow rushes past.

'You know. Sometimes kids grow up, and they don't realise. Things in the family aren't all hunky dory, but they don't quite get it, and they end up feeling responsible. And then when they look back as adults they can see it had nothing to do with them – there were a whole lot of other problems there.'

'What's that supposed to mean?'

'Only that there could have been something going on between the two of them, some dynamic you didn't have access to. Have you thought about that?'

Has she? She thinks of her Dad suddenly, the way when they were little he'd run to find them as soon as he came back from the evening train – *Will? Andrea? Where have those kids got to?* – clapping his hands. How he'd pull them down on either side of him on the sofa and listen as they told him about their day at school, while her mother busied herself determinedly with all the little kitchen tasks. How one evening much later, when she was a teenager, the time she was so worried about her IT coursework, she found her mum red-eyed in the bedroom. How neither of them said anything, how she'd found herself just mumbling something as she backed quickly out of the doorway. How when her dad got home he'd smoothed the text-book open on the table and looked her in the eye and said simply, *You can.* Her throat constricts.

'Andrea?'

'Mm?'

'Think about it.' Laura's still following doggedly on the lorry's tail. The car stinks of diesel. They're only doing about seventy-five.

'Look, Laura . . .' She tries hard to keep her voice steady.

'You know, women can't always be the kind of mothers they want. It's hard. I'm sure she loved you. You were adorable as a child. I know. You showed me the pictures, remember? She cared for you more than she cared for anyone. You probably saved her life.'

'How can you say that? You've barely even met her.' She almost jumps at the aggression in her own voice.

'I know *you*. And I can see this could be your last chance to talk with her and say goodbye. Can you afford to let it go?' Laura says.

'Listen to you!' She's laughing – an odd, forced laugh that doesn't sound like her at all. 'What do you know about it? Your own mother died when you were at university, you haven't got any children yourself, you're not even living with someone! I can't believe you can actually sit there and tell me how to manage my life!'

God, what's she said? Poor Laura. She waits for an answer but nothing comes. Laura's driving at the same steady pace. The names float past, the sign to the airport with its child's drawing of a plane, the kilometres gradually ticking away. How much farther? Eight kilometres? Five? In spite of the air-conditioning Laura's face is covered with little beads of sweat. Andrea sees her lift her right hand from the wheel and wipe the skin across her cheek-bones with one finger.

Well, it serves her right. How could she possibly have a clue? Things are so different in England – so tight and small and well-behaved – how could she possibly understand? All you'd see would be the good things, the subtlety and humour and politeness – you wouldn't really have a clue about what was underneath. And Americans can be so trusting: Laura really believes in goodness, in the beauty and explicability of the world. She can't seem to grasp the fact that it isn't actually good, or even evil – but only failing and irremediable and desperately sad. Laura talks sometimes about sadness. But it isn't what she thinks. It isn't a reaction to something that happens, that you learn to deal with and grieve about and get over: it's a sane adult person's response to the whole experience of living in the twenty-first century.

She can imagine what Laura sees of England: an unlikely collage of theatre and pedestrian shopping streets and seagulls, flowers and pubs and Lake Windermere and Anne Hathaway's cottage. Whereas what she's flying back to is an England of polystyrene litter and graffiti, drunks shouting abuse as they lurch home through the precinct, old people with bags of urine taped to their wasted calves. Her eyes fill with tears suddenly and she turns her face to the window. They're coming into the airport now. Rows of neat square trees slide past, every alternate one covered with purple blossom. What are they? You see them everywhere. I've been living here all these years and never even bothered to ask.

Laura swings the car into the car-park and brings it to a stop in the shade. Without looking at Andrea she turns off the engine and gets out to open the boot. She reaches in for the hold-all and puts it down in the grit at their feet.

Andrea looks at her watch. Twenty minutes to spare, after all that. She needn't have worried. She hoists the bag to her shoulder. 'Laura, I didn't—'

'You better go check in,' Laura says.

And what can she do about it anyway? She can't take the words back. And it's the truth. If Laura hasn't managed to face up to it by now it's about time she did. 'Bye, then.' The tears still won't stop trying to come. She shakes her head to clear them. 'See you soon.' She waits for Laura to put a reassuring hand on her arm but she doesn't. She doesn't even offer to carry the bag. She slides into the driving-seat and pulls the door shut and starts to back away.

The flight's an hour delayed. She checks the arrivals on the overhead screens and sees that the incoming plane hasn't even landed – it's probably only just leaving Gatwick. She feels in her bag for her book and sits with it in the upstairs café, reading each paragraph at least twice. It's a book about rural France – something Laura picked up somewhere – but it's crap. She finds herself getting more and more impatient. It's like something out of Country Living – all varnished wooden floors and walk-in fireplaces and quaint French customs. It's all so bloody comforting! To read this, you'd think everything had hardly changed – that the little villages are still buzzing with gentle, rural activity, the fields and vineyards the author refers to in passing as rich and prosperous as they ever were. But it's a myth, a con, an elaborate film-set. Walk into one of those little villages and you see the houses are crumbling – the ones that haven't been bought up and restored by Brits, anyway. Sometimes a whole wall's caved in and you can see inside to a derelict kitchen, the iron hooks above the hearth where they'd hang the pots and pans. The vineyards are shrinking slowly, the farming population aging and dying, the fields fusing together, napalmed into one enormous field.

She's hungry, she realises. It's more or less lunch-time,

and she had breakfast early, so as to be ready when Damien arrived. She buys herself a plastic container of *salade niçoise* and eats it slowly, watching the various flight details move up the screen. Paris, Amsterdam . . . The flights immediately before and after hers have been given gate numbers already. She reads a few more pages, without enthusiasm. Where are the French people she's known – the ones who have a way of interrupting you when you're searching for a word or phrase, the women who weave grimly through the market-day crowds, that student of hers who folds her sun-dried laundry into perfect little sharp-edged piles.

She's certainly got time for a coffee. She gets out her purse to search for change, tipping it slightly so the coins slide down into the leather tray. Something falls out, slithering across her palm and on to the surface of the table in a little rush. It's Laura's necklace, the one she bought at the market stall a few days ago. Andrea teases it out on the steel table-top, arranging the copper chain in a neat circle, turning the little shells over so they all face the same way.

Even in the plane, she's still thirsty. In the panic about Damien she'd forgotten to put in a bottle of water to drink in the car, and when she'd come through Security and had the chance to buy one she forgot again. When the steward comes down the aisle she catches his attention and asks him if she can buy some. The bottle he brings her is English, from some spa town in the North, very cold. She drinks half of it down quickly, gasping for breath. Through the window she can see the airfield, the brown grass moving slightly in the midday heat, another plane at the end of the runway, preparing to take off. Their own must be third in the queue.

She takes another mouthful of water and feels the cool of it travel down. That's better. Behind her on the ground Laura will be back at the house by now, the car already cooling in the dappled shade under the trees. She winces, remembering their conversation. But Laura won't take it badly – they've known each other so long, since they were students together on that summer course in Aix. Laura's used to her slightly unpredictable ways. She has the feeling that Laura would forgive her anything. Perhaps Laura's as close to her these days as her own mother – the only mother she has left.

The plane at the end of the runway revs its engines and starts to move forward, gathering speed, and another slides into view behind it, turning to point its nose in the same direction. Their own plane edges forward to where the second plane was. It's easy for Laura to pontificate. She's American. Things are easier in the U.S. You pick up a phone and ask someone to fix something and before you know it they come out and fix it for you. You don't automatically see your life as a long downhill slide into discomfort and despair. And Laura lost her mum so long ago now, and her dad's still fit and healthy – she hasn't even really had to think about all this yet. For her everything's more straightforward somehow: she isn't married; she's never even seemed very interested. She's got what sounds like a pretty cushy job teaching at that private university. She seems to be able to take off for the whole summer and make a show of working on some obscure French writer no one's ever heard of almost whenever she likes.

Now the second plane's roaring away. Behind it the edges of the runway ripple. She watches the landscape at the window change as their own cabin turns slowly through a hundred and eighty degrees. They stand waiting to take off. What was it they were talking about the other night at Pete's, that French couple Pete and Liz played tennis with – Chloë, was that what the woman's name was? Telling everyone the whole story of the nuclear power-station at Jumelech. What it was like, fifteen years ago, when the rumours first started. Then the arrival of the bulldozers. The great diggers and armies of men in hard hats, the cranes to hoist the concrete blocks into place as the two towers rose steadily from the flat space between the river and the canal. How some young student climbed the ladder and stayed up there for days, refusing to budge. How people in the village went round collecting signatures. But it didn't achieve anything. In the end they built it and started it up just the same. And it's true the town has so far done quite well out of it all. It was nuclear power-station money that bought new play equipment for the school and relandscaped the garden of the *asile de vieillards*, that paid for the new cobbles under the arcades in the town square. But somewhere in every house, in a bathroom cabinet or between the piles of embroidered pillow-cases in an oak armoire, or in a wicker basket on a tiled work-top, there's a packet of potassium capsules to be taken in the event of an emergency, 'to make the thyroid shut down'. 'So that we would not be another Chernobyl,' Philippe explained in English. 'And so far there has never been a problem. They have even made a kind of nice stairs for the fish.'

She shivers, reaching up to alter the direction of the air-conditioning nozzle slightly. What does it matter? None of it has any meaning. When she gets back to England, who knows what she'll be confronted with? It's too late for her mum, probably. At her age it's unlikely she'll ever be the person she was. It'll be a matter of being moved from bed to chair to commode to bed in some kind of canvas sling. She'll be fed and medicated and washed. Ankles swelling with fluid, arms folding in on themselves like a bird's wing. She'll have lost her glasses. She'll lose her words, her teeth, her hearing. It happens to everyone. You just have to live long enough. It's unbearable. And what difference does distance make? It's irrelevant. Laura simply doesn't have any conception of that. The fact of ageing and death is too overwhelming. Even if I do come back and live with Jim again in that house on the hill just above Champfleury, I'll always know this now.

The plane starts to rev its engines, its whole body vibrating. They're moving off down the runway. *The continuous labour of your life is to build the house of death*, who was it said that? Some old French geezer they forced you to read when you were at university – Montaigne, was it? It's consoling, in an odd kind of way. Another quote comes into her mind out of nowhere: *Poverty of goods is easily cured; poverty of soul, impossible*. Does she suffer from poverty of soul? Perhaps she does. Laura's right: if she can just – somehow – be sorry for messing things up with her mum, make up for what they've lost, be forgiven by someone. But it isn't possible. She only has to remember that last conversation they had, just before she moved here to France. *If you do go and live over there, it'll be as if I haven't got a daughter*. Could she really have said that?

She catches a glimpse of blurred grass, the edge of the runway speeding past, and then the plane starts to lift. Beyond the wing-tip the ground reels away, the fields fanning out and shrinking quickly from ochre to a bluish haze, the darker blue of the woods spread out between them like lakes. For a moment she sees herself falling, straight down until she hits the surface, the cool surrounding her as she slows rapidly in a rush of bubbles and then begins to swim up. But it's okay. After a while the plane levels off and she can see the river glinting as it curls round a field striped with trees. She sits forward in her seat to try and get a glimpse of Aubrillac with its little square of covered arcades, but they're too high up, she can't make out anything except this gentle landscape of forest and farmland stretching to the horizon. But then in the bottom left-hand corner of her window the power-plant swims into view, its two great cooling-towers like two open mouths, the steam from one of them casting a little trail of shadow that breaks into pieces and moves slowly away across the baked earth.

SUSIE

Perhaps it was possible to get back some of what she'd lost since Jim left? If not the outings and dinners with the other couples they used to be friends with, then at least some of the little things she used to enjoy for herself. Okay, so she never managed to get Jim to build them a pool. But there was still this fantastic space out the back, smooth and rippling with tree-shadows, almost as inviting as a pool would have been. She could come out here for a few minutes every day and start meditating again. She'd hardly had time to meditate for a single second since Jade was born.

She'd felt a bit uncomfortable about mentioning it to Alex at first. It didn't seem like something she ought to be paying someone to look after Jade for. But Alex had just grinned at her and said, 'Go for it.' She was an odd kid. Sometimes she came out with the exact opposite of what you expected. And she could be surprisingly intuitive. It was almost as if she could see right inside you sometimes – even when you were doing your very utmost to cover up how you really felt. She could tell when you were feeling a bit down, even if you'd hardly opened your mouth. You must be giving out some kind of aura and she was somehow managing to pick it up.

Susie tried to clear her mind. *Let go.* From here under the overhang of the old barn the slope of the lawn with its patterns of light and shade was just gorgeous. The grass still had a mist of dew on it, it seemed to be crying out for your bare feet. The murmur of voices reached her on the breeze from next door's garden – Murielle's rising like a question, sounding slightly aggressive as she always did, even when she was obviously perfectly happy; Didier answering her from time to time in a low rumble. And then Alex, a bit hesitant, speaking to one or other of them in her careful schoolgirl French. Water hissing from the hose and dripping down between the wet leaves.

Let go. Her mind was a tree, and the tree had thousands of branches. At the end of each little twig leaf-buds opened gently, twisting and bursting in the sunlight under her skull. Her whole mind was reaching upwards and outwards towards the sun, towards the faint line of mountains she could just see on the horizon, the invisible planets circling out there beyond the blue. She heard a sudden squeal and came back to herself with a shiver. Jade must have put out her hand and touched the fine spray of water, bless her. There was a clip-clipping noise from where Didier was standing on his step-ladder just on the other side of the hedge. In the distance she could hear a dustcart somewhere over in the village – by those stinking rubbish skips in the car-park, probably – beeping as it reversed, crunching the plastic bags of waste.

What had happened to the sunlit tree? She tried to get it back but it wasn't that easy. What was it her horoscope said this week? That she was going to meet someone interesting who'd change the whole direction of her life? Well, where was he? He'd better turn up soon – it was halfway through the week already and as far as she could see there were only all the usual suspects; she hadn't been introduced to anyone new. If he was really going to be here before the weekend he'd better start getting his act together. It could be like . . . She saw a sudden picture of Alex, the expression in her eyes that day Jack came to the kitchen door to ask if she wanted to go over. Crazy about each other, both of them, you could tell. She breathed in deeply and let the air out of her lungs again in a long sigh. It was how things ought to be at their age. It was how they were between her and Jim at the beginning. They should make the most of it, she kept telling them. Once that first fizzy feeling had gone you hardly ever got it back.

The tree . . . shivered in the breeze and put out another few leaves, stirring towards a haze of sunlight. Clip. Clip. She remembered suddenly that some of the essential oils she used needed replacing. She was almost out of clary-sage, she'd noticed a few days ago, and the sandalwood was getting quite low. And there was nowhere around here that stocked them at all, it was really quite primitive in some ways, she had to get them by mail order from a place she'd found back in England. And by the time she could get herself together to write out the order and find an envelope and address it, it'd be midday already, the Champfleury post office shut. *Rats.* That village post office really was pathetic. It might as well not be there really – it was never open when you needed it. The old guy who ran it never seemed to keep it open a minute longer than he had to – though you couldn't exactly blame him: he'd been looking really thin and ill some mornings lately. No doubt he had problems of his own. She wouldn't want to be mean. But she'd arrived on the doorstep sometimes to find the door shut in her face – at one minute past twelve!

Doors. She closed her eyes and saw Jim standing in the

bedroom doorway, his hand flat against the frame. Even from where she'd been lying under the bedclothes she could smell the alcohol on his breath. *Do you even make enough to live on? You're just pretending to be alive.* For a second she felt light-headed, her life tipping away from her in a lurch of shame and helplessness. What was he trying to do? But then her mind took control, grasping the angry figure of Jim and pushing it away, making it smaller. A blink and it was smaller still, a little man shouting and gesticulating to himself in the doorway of some distant bedroom no bigger than a room in a dolls' house. Somewhere infinitely far away from her, her husband was jeering and waving his hands. Then he went quiet. He turned himself round stiffly and walked back down the stairs and out the way he'd come.

Well, it was a beginning anyway. She uncrossed her legs and rolled up the mat. Later, when she was driving into Aubrillac, she thought of it again and smiled. Inside her skull something still waved yellow and green. Momentarily she saw the same image of Jim, his hand lowered to his side and clenching. She focused hard until she could see the way the grubby denim had faded over his thighs, the way the flesh just over the bridge of his nose gathered itself into little vertical pleats. Then she shrank it to the size of a golf-ball, a walnut, a marble, a pea. He was like a miniature – something tiny and delicately crafted you might see and fall in love with and buy someone as a gift. His size 11 feet were so dainty! She almost burst out laughing.

She stopped in the car-park at the cross-roads, near the Hôtel de l'Horloge with its shady tables under the plane-trees, and went into the town post-office to post her order. And who should be there but the American woman, about three places ahead of her in the queue, with a large parcel in her arms.

For a moment she was tempted to walk out. Bumping into some crazy American was all she needed. But it was too late – already the woman had seen her and waved. And when she'd done her business at the counter she was actually there just outside the door, waiting. 'How you doing?' Laura said. Her hand was on Susie's back. 'Do you have time for a coffee?'

Susie glanced at her watch.

'Do you have to go somewhere?'

'No, it's . . .' She tried to find some gentle excuse. She wouldn't want to hurt the woman's feelings. And it was a bad idea to get too friendly with a client, it felt awkward afterwards, when you met them in your professional role. But her mind seemed to have gone blank.

'Here?' Laura waved her hand towards the hotel terrace with its white linen tables.

It looked horribly expensive, the kind of place where you'd sit primly with your legs crossed and cock your little finger as you lifted the handle of a bone china coffee-cup. In the evenings it was full of slim, bronzed French couples, the women showing their brown shoulders, pushing their hair back behind their neat ears. She said, 'How about down by the river? That little café on the corner, near where they rent out the bikes?'

'Sounds good,' Laura said.

They plonked themselves at the table farthest from the door. Down at the end of the street she could see a little section of river sparkling.

'Do you think they have iced tea?' Behind her sunglasses

Laura's eyes were invisible. She somehow managed to look really un-European. Was it her hair? Something about the cut of her beige linen trousers? Or the comfortable-looking openwork design of her leather shoes?

'Do they do iced tea in France?'

'Sometimes.'

She felt suddenly reckless. 'I'll have a glass of rosé,' she found herself saying. 'If that's all right. It's such ages since I've sat in a café like this, just to talk.'

'Sure.' Laura was smiling at her – a big, encouraging smile. 'My pleasure.' She beckoned the café owner over and gave her order in fluent French. Where on earth did she learn that from? She sounded almost like a native. When he'd gone she turned back to Susie and said, 'No iced tea, alas. I ordered a carafe of Brulhois for the two of us. So . . . what was it that made you decide to come and live in France?'

And before she knew it she was telling Laura everything – the dreams she'd had about the old farmhouse, the barn with its wonderful roof sloping almost to the ground, the grass behind, the village, everything. How she'd got started with the alternative therapies – the people she'd met, the books she'd ordered. How from tiny beginnings her little business had grown and grown, so that now it was almost capable of supporting her – herself and Jade – as long as nothing unexpected happened – as long as nothing decided to burn out or leak or break down. 'And then . . .' She tailed off, the fact of Laura's friendship with Andrea hitting her suddenly.

Laura's face was turned towards the little stretch of water. Susie followed the direction of her eyes to where the sun fell on the centre of the stream, breaking up into flakes. The light almost hurt to look at. Laura turned back to face her. 'Now doesn't that look great?' She pulled down her sunglasses and peered at Susie over the top of the brown plastic frames. 'What do you say we go down there and rent a canoe?'

'What?' She'd hardly even been in a rowing-boat, let alone something as wobbly-looking as a canoe.

'C'mon.' Laura pushed back her chair and went inside to pay the bill. She came out almost at once, slinging the strap of her leather bag over her shoulder. 'He says we pay his son, down there on the quay.'

She couldn't believe she was doing this – that she'd actually let some crazy American talk her into sitting in this fragile man-made shell and stirring the water with a great flat tea-spoon. Her dress was up round her thighs, marked with dark splashes; her arms were already shiny with sweat.

But once you'd got over the laughter and embarrassment and stopped worrying about going in a straight line, it really was fantastic. All round them the willows wept. At their feet in the still surface another row wept upwards to meet them. And the shallow hull cut smoothly across, through a dark brown-blue sky dotted with floating leaves.

They hardly knew each other. The two of them only met a few days ago. But something about the easy swing of Laura's back as she paddled them forwards seemed to tell Susie she'd got it wrong. Laura wasn't the nerdy blue-stocking she'd imagined. There was actually more to her than you'd have thought. She handled the paddle as if she'd been doing it since childhood, dipping the blade rhythmically and raising it in a sparkle of drops, the muscles of her back tensing and releasing. Susie hardly had to do a thing. After a while she leaned against the fibreglass back-rest and let Laura take the strain. She tipped her face backwards and closed her eyes, feeling the shadows rippling over her skin.

They travelled a long way downriver. After a while they rounded a bend to see a smaller, second weir and Susie felt herself clutch the sides of the boat, her heart beating in her temples. But it was all right. There was a little arrow telling you where to point the front of your canoe. Laura angled them expertly towards it and they slipped down a narrow rush of white water to bob, turning slightly, towards the edge of the leafy pool underneath. A few more bends and they were stuck in shallows and facing backwards, their keel caught on a submerged rock. Laura rolled up her trousers and waded in and heaved the prow round until they were adrift again, pointing in the right direction. From the launching-place just below the big weir they'd come what seemed like several miles already. Sometimes Laura put up her own paddle and let them drift with the current, just dipping it in occasionally and giving it a little wiggle when they threatened to go into the bank. After a while they got to the perfect place. She watched as Laura leaned to loop the rope round a tree-trunk and knot it firmly, pulling herself out on to a grassy tussock and steadying the canoe with her foot, as she held out her hand. She really had been doing this for years. Susie let herself be half-dragged up the bank, stumbling on the uneven ground and almost falling into Laura's arms. Laura was grinning at her. 'There you go.'

'Thanks.'

They sat together in a tent of shade, the branches so low they brushed the surface. The hanging fronds were yellow with sunlight. Between them she could just see the water, a narrow leaf turning with the current as it slid past. 'Now, isn't this amazing?' Laura said. 'You come somewhere like this and you feel different almost immediately. You find yourself wondering where all that weight of grief and sorrow came from, what that was all about.'

'Have you got grief?'

'No, not really.' Laura shook her head and a strand of hair fell across her eyes. It was almost auburn. She pushed it back. 'Well, yeah. I suppose in a way I do.'

'About your research?'

Laura turned and looked at her. 'My research? Gaston Philippe, you mean? Oh, no. He's dead, he's not temperamental, you can always depend on him to tell you the whole truth – if you know how to read him, that is.' She hesitated, studying the water at their feet. An electric blue dragonfly nosed between the tree-roots and then lifted off again like a helicopter. A small raft of weed and twigs bobbed in under the bank, caught against something and hung motionless for a moment before breaking away. 'I just drove a friend to the airport this morning. She's visiting her mom back in England. I guess she was somewhat . . . confused.'

'Did she hurt your feelings?'

Laura looked up in surprise. 'My feelings?'

'Well . . .'

Laura said, 'Andrea and I go back a long way.'

Susie combed the long grass with her left hand. 'How did you meet?'

'We were on a study program together, in Aix-en-Provence. My mother had recently been killed in an automobile accident. Andrea was so good to me then.'

In spite of the warmth Susie shivered. 'That must have been awful – for you and your . . . father.' She heard herself say, 'I do know Andrea actually. I should have said. Jim's my husband – or ex-husband, whatever you like to call it. We haven't really had time yet to call it anything. She's the woman he left me to shack up with.' She felt herself starting to blush. 'She does strike me as a bit . . .' God, why had she started on this whole thing about Andrea, how could she possibly go on? Laura was looking at her, waiting.

'Confused?'

Susie's eyes filled with tears suddenly. Shit. The trees on the opposite bank were a blur. She concentrated on keeping her voice level as she said, 'She's a lot more into books and art and all that sort of thing than I am. I didn't even think about going to university when I was a teenager, I was just into clothes and boys and having fun. And Jim's a sucker for a bit of culture. You know he started off as a teacher, before he got into the pool thing?'

Laura said, 'I didn't know that.' An insect settled on the back of her hand and she brushed it off.

There was a twig lying right next to Susie's foot. She reached for it and started breaking it into little pieces. 'But she hurt your feelings.'

For a moment Laura didn't answer. The skin at the corners of her eyes crinkled. She said, 'You know, I get the sense that things between them aren't always that great.'

'Is he drinking again?'

Laura turned the full beam of her attention towards Susie suddenly, shading her eyes with her hand. She said, 'That must have been really tough, when you and Jim split up. And you have a child, right?'

She nodded. For a moment she didn't trust herself to speak. From somewhere behind them and far over to their left, the murmur of what must be the town came faintly across the fields. 'It was just when the pool business was starting to take off really. Things ought to have been getting easier. I'm not sure what went wrong.' She touched parts of her own mind tentatively, like probing a painful tooth with her tongue. No one had ever bothered to ask her about it until now. After a while she said, 'Laura?'

'Uh-huh?'

'Do you believe in spirit?'

'How d'you mean?'

'Something you can't see or hear but only feel – something that's in everything, or behind everything? That stays alive in the next generation when we're gone?'

'Sure I do.'

It sounded so matter-of-fact. Could she be serious? Susie squinted up at the sky, trying to find the words. Above the chestnut trees on the opposite bank a plume of white smoke waved from one of the Jumelech towers, unexpectedly close. 'So . . . with all the books you've read, all your education . . .' she said finally, tailing off in embarrassment.

But Laura was still smiling. 'With all my education . . . what?' she said, and laughed.

'You still don't think there's necessarily a scientific explanation for everything in our lives?'

Without bothering to take off her sunglasses Laura rubbed across her eyes with one hand. The frames lifted and fell back on her nose, lop-sided. 'Like what?'

'Like us. Me and Jim. You. Andrea. And the future – my little girl, Jade – the way their lives will be after we've gone?'

'Well, Gaston Philippe certainly didn't think there was. He was seriously into all those things, all kinds of weird phenomena that weren't exactly religious, but couldn't be readily accounted for either. Coincidences. Chains of events that don't seem entirely random and yet appear to be set off totally by chance. He thought a lot about something he called "the pilgrimage without belief".'

'How interesting,' she said politely.

'Yeah. He was.' Laura ran the flat of her hand over the sandy soil between them. She looked up suddenly and smiled. 'You just go.'

'What?'

'You go. Like going off hiking. You start out in the morning when it's still cool, carry your back-pack up the hill, up on to the plateau – whether you have any real belief or not, it doesn't matter. You just wake up in the morning and pack up your stuff and put it on your back and go. And in the evening when you come down to the next village and hear the church clock chiming seven, you rest. It's that simple. It's as complicated and simple as that.'

What was it about this woman? As Susie listened a huge, choking mass of something seemed to rise from her stomach so she could hardly speak. Jim and Andrea, Alex, Jade – they were all in there somewhere, all churning round in a kind of gigantic flood or shipwreck, she could feel and taste them all. Her eyes filled again with tears. Laura reached out and touched her shoulder and before she knew it she'd turned towards her. She was sobbing like a child in Laura's arms.

'It's okay, it's okay,' Laura kept saying.

And you could almost believe it was. The warmth of her hug was so genuine, she was an amazing woman, it almost made you want to throw in your whole hand and start again. Perhaps, even now, it would be possible to have a completely different kind of life. This old geezer Laura was always going on about, she could be like him. She could just see him. He'd be like one of the hikers sitting around that hut on the village green, spreading pâté on a baguette with a Swiss army knife and sprawling in the shade to eat it, watching her and Jade go past through the two grey slits of his eyes. After a while she stopped crying and felt in her pocket for a tissue to mop her face. 'I'm so sorry.'

'It's okay,' Laura said again. 'It happens to everyone. It's okay.'

'It's got so bad lately. I have to do this visualisation exercise.'

'Excuse me?'

'I have to imagine them – Jim and Andrea – I have to get a clear picture. Then I make them smaller and smaller, till they're so tiny they actually seem to shrink away.'

'They do?' Laura raised her eyebrows. She started to laugh. 'That's wonderful! What a gloriously simple solution! Susie, you know what?'

Susie shook her head.

'It's great. You've found a way of dealing with all kinds of shit – global warming, terrorism, natural disasters, Afghanistan, you name it. You don't even have to do anything. You just see it in your mind's eye and *voilà*!' She waved her hand theatrically towards the far bank. The line of poplars shivered, the tops picked out in sun. 'You can shrink away the problems of the whole world.' She pushed her sunglasses up into her hair and pressed the heels of her hands into her eyes. When she took them away she was still laughing.

And Susie was laughing with her. It was hopeless. The whole long, glorious afternoon was breaking up around them into bright flakes of leaf and dragonfly and water and sun. Whoever this woman was, she'd never met anyone quite like her. Even her laugh was something special – generous and uninhibited. If anyone knew about spirit she did. Susie found herself looking at her with something embarrassingly like admiration. She'd almost forgotten what happiness felt like. This was the first time she'd really laughed since before Jim left.

Somewhere up-river a church clock struck. Laura looked up, frowning. The shadows of the trees on the grass were longer than they had been.

Susie asked, 'What time was that?' She must have forgotten to put on her watch. After a couple of minutes it came again. They both listened, counting.

'My God!' Laura said.

'Was it *five*?'

'Yup.'

'What time do we have to get the canoe back?'

'Six.'

She watched the current swirling gently past, a crumpled cigarette-packet out in the middle of the stream. Marlboro. 'Can we make it?'

'You bet.' Laura was already stepping down into the canoe, stretching out her hand to help her to follow, reaching to untie the rope. It slithered into the water with a soft plop. Drops ran off it, glistening in the slanting sunlight as her strong arms pulled it up and coiled it in a neat circle, looping it round the metal thing at the front.

It was a long way back. They'd been paddling for what seemed like hours already and there was no way of telling how far they'd come or how far they still had to go. She rested her paddle across the top of the canoe and leaned forward onto it, as she'd seen the men in the boat race do at the end. 'I'm sorry, Laura. I can't do this any more.'

'Yeah, you can.' Laura was still paddling doggedly. They *were* still making progress against the current, however slow. She watched a clump of rushes inch its way past. 'You just have to let your mind drift. Think of something else.'

'Like what?'

'Like . . . uh, I don't know. Whatever your personal equivalent of Gaston Philippe is.'

Her first thought was that she hadn't got anyone or anything of her own. But of course she had: she'd got Jade – her little dimpled hands and the back of her neck, the tiny, silky wisps of hair that tickled your skin. Her little toes, fresh from the bath. The whole smell and feel of her. She was changing so quickly now, learning new things every day. What was that funny sound she's made only this morning? Like a bumble-bee or passing tractor, her lips vibrating, wet with spit. She'd done it over and over again. Susie started to smile.

Somehow she managed to go on paddling. In front of her Laura worked at the same pace, not even looking tired. She seemed to remember where the deeper channels were. At the weir they lifted the canoe out and carried it between them without even thinking to complain. By the time the church clock over in Champfleury struck six it sounded a bit nearer than it had been. When they heard it strike six again they were just passing the first houses, clustered together under the trees at the edges of the town. 'You see?' Laura said.

'We're not there yet.'

'But almost.'

'And it's gone six already.'

'Oh . . .' Laura turned her head and grinned. 'They're southerners, right? They won't care about the extra fifteen minutes.'

And it seemed she knew them better than they did themselves. When the white curtain of the big weir came into view, they could see Théo sitting on the wall waiting for them next to the quay, his long legs stretched out in front of him, crossed at the ankle. He smiled at them as they drew level. 'So. Did you have a good afternoon?' He reached for the rope and guided the prow in next to the others.

Susie said, 'We're a bit late. I'm sorry.'

Théo shook his head, spreading his fingers, palms downwards. 'Don't mention it.'

'Can we give you something?' Laura was reaching for her wallet.

But he shook his head again. 'You brought back the canoe. That's the main thing.' He tied the boat up next to the others and gave Susie a brief wave before trudging uphill towards the café. What a lovely young man he was. She saw him disappearing at the corner of her eye.

She felt embarrassed suddenly. She ought to say something to Laura to let her know just how special this whole afternoon had been. But what? It was so hard when you'd been really touched by something, it was almost impossible to find the right words. 'Laura?'

'Yeah?'

You know, I don't often . . . No. *This really was* . . . She stood stupidly, her mind full of meaningless phrases. She swallowed. 'Laura, I don't expect . . . I mean . . . I was wondering . . . ?'

Laura bent her head, fiddling with her sunglasses. She

reached into her bag for the case and slipped them inside.
When she looked up she was smiling. 'We should do something like this again, you mean? Sure. I'd like that.'

'So . . . ?' Her voice tailed off, croaky and childish.

'You know, the cottage I'm renting isn't so close to Jim
and Andrea's house. And Andrea's away now anyway. And
Jim's hardly ever there. Why don't you come up Thursday?
We can have lunch.'

MAGALI

Even before she gets to the café she can hear the shouting coming from inside. She stands a few metres away, just under the tiled overhang of the old market, and watches the shadows move in the lit shape of the open doorway. 'But, Dad!' she hears Théo say. 'It wasn't my fault, Dad! I keep telling you.' And the whine of Jeannine's voice in the background. And then Théo's again: 'Dad, they were supposed to come back at six! What do you expect me to do, call up the fire brigade?'

But Maurisse obviously isn't having any. His voice is louder than Théo's – he doesn't care who hears him. 'I thought you'd be able to manage that at least. It's not much to ask. Just to get yourself up here on time and give me a bit of a hand before the evening rush starts.'

'I did give you a hand. And it wasn't that late. The evening rush hadn't started.'

'I don't know what you think you'll be good for this time next year when you haven't got that school to fall back on. Not this kind of work, obviously. You're not responsible enough. You can't even manage to keep track of a couple of canoes! How can you run a business if you're off in the clouds

somewhere and letting your customers treat you like shit?
And look at you – they could take off all night and you'd still
be there at the quayside waiting like a stupid jug!'

She winces on Théo's behalf. But it isn't over. Now Jeannine's joining in again, louder this time, gaining confidence
as she works herself up. 'You spend far too much time with
that girl lately, that's the trouble. You can't be bothered with
anyone but her. No wonder you can't manage to do even the
simplest little job without making a complete mess of it. She's
turned you into a half-wit. I don't know what she sees in
you. And she's not doing her own family any favours either.
I bet her own mother could do with some help, what with
the old man and the two younger ones, not to mention all
those hordes of cousins who keep coming over to see them
from Agen. About time she gave a bit of thought to her own
family for a change.' A shadow darkens the doorway and she
sees Théo's hand part the plastic ribbons.

'Théo!' It's Maurisse's voice.

'What?'

'I'll see to the bikes and canoes from now on. You can help
your mother clear up in the café. We'll see how it goes for
a couple of months. Show us you can be sensible and we'll
think about it again.'

She shrinks back into the shadow of the covered market
as Théo pushes out and past, head down, his hands in his
pockets. He doesn't turn down Rue des Menuisiers but carries
on round the edge of the square to the opposite corner, his
footsteps echoing on the cobbles. His slim back disappears
between two buildings. He must be heading for the As de
Coeur, over on the other side of the church. The Horloge
would be too expensive, and anyway he's not dressed for it.

She wanders down towards the dark river, playing the whole melodramatic scene over again in her head. It's incredible. It's like they're stuck in a time-warp, still saying the kind of stuff people said to her own mother thirty years ago. Can there possibly be any truth in it? Is she a bad influence on him? Perhaps she is. From their point of view anyway. And yet she only wants what's best for him. It's just that what's best in her eyes isn't likely to be what's best in theirs. *Families, I hate you.* Who was it said that? All she wants for the two of them is that they should both get out of here eventually and find something . . . well, bigger. Something she hasn't got the experience yet even to imagine. But she's read books, she's had a glimpse of it occasionally on TV, she remembers the look in M Briot's eyes as he tried to tell them: what you see here isn't all there is.

But it's hard. She knows what her own mother would say. *It's about quality of life.* It's good to live simply. People in the cities have lost any feeling for the really important things. They live in small boxes, working at routine office jobs day in day out to get money for clothes and entertainments. If they're lucky they earn enough to buy a car and a small new house in the suburbs. They go on holiday to the Mediterranean, the Caribbean even. They go skiing in January or February and come back with panda eyes. They don't even bother to cook properly any more, or go to Mass. Out here you can still bring up your kids in peace and safety. You can grow your own tomatoes and breathe clean air and live more or less as your grandparents did.

But it's all old talk. Her mum's old. Someone her age doesn't remember what it's like to stand next to a boy and feel your body turn to water. Someone her age doesn't have dreams or ambitions any more. At the bottom of the steps that lead down to the little quay the boats bob gently. The lights from the road on the other side wobble in the water. In the tree over her head a cricket starts up its high-pitched churring, like the wheel of a bike being turned backwards.

It's really late. But she has to see him. She stands in the shadow of the café wall and listens. She can hear a TV on in a room somewhere at the back. And there's a light on upstairs, in the room they call 'le vérandah', the room with two glass walls and a bank of window-boxes, flowers tumbling down red and pink and orange over her head. She's been up there with Théo once or twice – in her mind's eye she sees a round table covered with a mustard-yellow cloth, a clothes-horse draped with tea-towels and pillow-cases, a white glass ashtray at the right elbow of the green plastic chair Maurisse uses for his afternoon nap. Théo's shape passes across the glass and she wills him to look down.

He seems to feel it and comes to the window. He peers down at her over a frill of petunias. 'Magali?'

She steps out away from the wall so the light from the lamp falls directly into her eyes. He says, 'I'll come down.' He pulls his head back, ready to disappear towards the door.

'No!' She shakes her head and puts her finger to her lips.

'What's the matter?'

A small Siamese cat appears from nowhere and pads slowly through the shaft of light, pausing and lifting its head to her as it goes past, its fur almost the same colour as the walls, its eyes a clear, pale blue. 'I heard,' she says. 'I heard it all.'

'You did?' His face hangs there looking at her for a moment. 'Well, it was a complete load of shit. I don't give a fuck about any of it. They live in another world.'

Her voice shakes as she says, 'Perhaps I *am* a bad influence. From their point of view, maybe I am.'

'Magali?' His leaning face is in darkness and she can't see his expression. 'Are you serious? What are you trying to say?'

'I don't know.' She shakes her head. It's her fault. She's spoiling his life. She can taste salt at the back of her throat. 'I do . . . You know I do . . .' She swallows and twists her head away, out of the light. 'But I can't help it. My life has to be something more than this.'

'We'll make it more. We'll go somewhere else, together. Live somewhere on our own.'

He's crazy. At her feet there's a broken spray of begonia flowers, like a trail of blood. She bends to pick it up.

'We'll run a bike shop. I told you.'

'But . . .' Her voice sounds like his, when he's been smoking too many fags.

'What?'

'That's what you've got here, a fucking bike shop. I want something else.'

'Like what?'

She says quietly, 'I want to go to the university.'

'You can go to university. I'll run the shop and you can be a student. You can get a job in the evenings to tide us over just till we're on our feet.'

Does he know what he's saying? Does he even understand how much two people need to live on in the city? He's such a kid sometimes. 'Théo, I—'

'Magali, I can't go without you.'

Her legs go weak again as she remembers the afternoon in the dove-shoot hide, how he ran his fingers over her body till the walls seemed to open, how when he was inside her all the practical problems melted away; how there was nothing then but his face and his hands and the smell of his skin and the feel of him inside her, a feeling like drinking, a long, long gasp of clear water, tasting of *ah* and *yes*. She can still hear the birds singing under the old trees.

'Listen.' He's leaning out towards her so the glow from the street-lamp catches the front of his dark hair, turning it to copper. 'Meet me down by the river in a couple of hours' time.'

'What?' From here she can just read the figures on the church clock. Six minutes past eleven. 'Are you completely out of your mind?'

'Just do it.' His voice sounds suddenly different, more determined; it could be an adult speaking. 'Go home. Get your things. Be back here in two hours.'

Could he possibly be right? Is this what you have to do when you truly love someone – just go for it and leave all the details to take care of themselves? She says, 'How can it possibly work?'

'It will if we want it enough.'

'And I can still do my thing?'

'If that's what you want.'

He sounds so sure. She twirls the begonia between her fingers.

'We'll talk properly in a couple of hours. Go back and get your stuff. Don't wake anyone – don't give anything away. Trust me,' he says.

She nods and starts to walk. From the back of the café there's a roar of canned laughter, broken off abruptly as someone presses a button. When she turns to look she can still just see him, a dark shadow over the bank of flowers, watching her walk the length of the street.

When she gets to the river he's already waiting. His dark shape detaches itself from the trunk of one of the plane-trees and comes forward to meet her. 'Did you get your stuff?'

She nods. She's hardly brought anything. Just her bank card and her toilet bag, her underwear and a change of clothes. She hardly dares think of what she's left behind – the frilled cotton skirt she bought one day early in the summer from a stall in the market, the First Communion photo with her sister, the little wreath of porcelain flowers her Dad gave her about a year before he left. It was as much as she could do to squeeze in the paperback. She leans into him and he puts his arms round her. She stands for a moment in silence, feeling his warm breath in her hair. She can't believe she just went back home in the middle of the night and threw a few things together and left without even saying goodbye. Boy was the only one who seemed to sense something was going on: he'd licked her hand without whining or rattling his chain. She'd heard her grand-dad snoring from the ground floor bedroom next to the kitchen, Pauline's regular breathing in the back room upstairs. She'd tiptoed past her mother's door, her shoes in her hand. But she needn't have worried. They all slept like dormice. She'd grabbed at a few necessities and closed the door behind her softly. It would be hours yet before they even realised she was gone. 'I didn't have time for much.' She shows him the little purple and magenta rucksack she's brought – the child's backpack she used to carry her lunch in when she was at primary school.

It was the only thing she could lay hands on quickly without making any noise.

'You won't need much. We're not going to be on some desert island. We can buy what we need when we get there.'

She wants to say, 'And what are we going to use for cash?' but she's given up arguing with him. 'So.' She separates herself gently from his arms. 'What now? Do we hitch or walk?'

'Neither.'

'But there isn't—'

He puts a finger to her lips and she realises she's raised her voice. He feels for something in his pocket and beckons her over to a low door in the wall.

'What—?'

'Shh.' He turns the key in the lock and disappears into the shadows. Somewhere inside a weak light flicks on. A moment later he emerges, wheeling a bike. He gestures to her to hold it steady while he fetches another. She watches him re-lock the door and slide the key carefully into an envelope. He licks the flap and presses it down with his thumb, then disappears up the steep street, leaving her standing with a bicycle in each hand. A moment later he's taking one of them from her and leaning it against a tree-trunk to shrug on his backpack. Then they're on their way.

For the first couple of hundred metres they walk, the wheels quietly ticking over the cobbles. Then they mount and start to pedal, gathering speed. It takes them only a few minutes to shake off the town and they're in open country, whizzing along between orchards of green apples and fields of man-high corn. And suddenly she wants to start singing, shouting, anything. They've done it. They can go anywhere, do anything. Her dynamo casts a faint yellow arc on the tarmac in front of her handlebars and she can follow it wherever it takes her, flying on and on half-blind into the dark.

They free-wheel almost soundlessly through Champfleury and take the lane on the left, out towards Seyrac. He's cycling ahead of her, even though she's the only one with lights. She can see his dark back swaying between the verges like some kind of mythical animal on delicate legs – a centaur, is it? – and she wants to laugh. 'Théo, wait for me! Where are we going?' He lets his bike glide to a stop and puts one foot down on the loose gravel at the verge.

He turns to look back at her, his face a pale oval against the apple-trees under their veils of shadowy netting. 'To Seyrac, where do you think? This road doesn't go anywhere else.'

'But—'

'They've gone away. I heard that American woman talking. The wife's mother's ill and they've gone back to look after her. I heard her telling that other English woman with the baby. They were going on about it yesterday afternoon when they were renting a canoe. They didn't realise I could understand what they were saying.'

'Right,' she says uncertainly. 'So we can turn on all the outside lights and play ping-pong all night, is that what you're saying?'

'All night?' She can tell he's grinning at her in the darkness. 'Fine by me. But I don't think we'll need the lights.'

When they turn the corner she begins to relax. The old farmhouse is in complete darkness, all the front shutters closed. All the same, about a hundred metres from the house they dismount and leave the bikes at the edge of an orchard, propped against the trunk of a tree. Together they walk quietly round to where the pool lies under its skin of nylon sheeting and climb over the low wall.

There's no sign of the battery-driven drill thing you're meant to use to take the cover off. They kneel, one on either side, and ease the heavy roll back on itself, one steel rib at a time. A slit of water appears and grows steadily wider, a sleepy eye dragging itself open. And almost before they've finished she's stripped and sliding down under the surface, feeling the cool of it on the back of her neck, her face, her crown, and coming up gasping, moving her arms and legs gently to keep herself afloat. She hears his voice from the other side, 'How is it?'

'Come in and find out!'

He's slipped in beside her. They're like two fish, naked and slippery. He kisses her and they almost go under. She feels his erect penis against her belly and guides it into her, clinging to him with her legs round his waist. After a while she feels her whole body turn to water, her face in the valley of his wet neck.

He's even managed to bring food. They pull on their clothes and picnic at the edge of the pool, guessing at what's inside the different packages from their size and shape – bread and duck liver pâté, apricots, a plastic bottle of wine. And when they've had enough they clear it all up and bundle it into his rucksack and pick their way towards the black archway of the garage barn. She bumps into him in the dark and he drops the shirt he's carrying, and she can't help it, she's nuzzling up to his cool, chlorine-scented skin, she wants to start all over again. And neither of them can stop laughing. They've actually done it, they've really managed to get away somewhere where they can be alone at last! They squeeze past the car in the barn and feel for the rungs of the old wooden ladder. In a moment they're up there on the boards, stretched out together in front of the ox-eye window. They've even made a bed for themselves by pulling loose handfuls out of a disintegrating bale of hay.

Has she ever felt this happy? If she has, she can't remember where or when. Through the little round window she can see a scattering of stars, like pale freckles on the dark blue. Out here it's like at home, there's no light pollution. In Aubrillac everything's lit up artificially for the tourists, every last cobble gleaming in the orange glow. And when they get to the city it'll be something else again. That's something she'll have to get used to. But it won't be too difficult. He's right – now they're together she can do anything. She'll enrol at the University, it doesn't cost that much. And she'll find a way. She'll go to lectures and read all day and be a waitress at some little restaurant in the evenings. And when she comes home he'll be there waiting. This crazy existence of escaping and making love and laughing will go on and on.

They're woken by whistling. Théo turns over and opens his eyes. 'Wha—?'

She puts her hand over his mouth. 'Shh!' She feels his long body tense against hers. They lie without moving as the whistling comes nearer, accompanied by footsteps on the gravel. Somewhere beneath the floorboards there's a clunk. The footsteps change tone as whoever it is enters the barn. There's the sound of a car door opening and slamming shut. A moment's silence and then the engine starts up, revving and reversing slowly out from under them, turning on the sweep of gravel in front of the house and easing down to the gate and out into the lane. Already it's fading in the distance. Théo sits up. There's a little patch of sunlight on his right cheekbone. She follows the shaft upwards between the rafters to what must be a chink between two tiles. She sneezes. The air around them's swimming with motes of dust and hay.

He's looking at her. He says slowly, '*Putain!*'

'They were here all the time!'

'And we . . .' His face is so comical that in spite of herself she starts to laugh again.

She sits up, brushing hay from her hair and clothes, then crouches at the little window. Under them a circle of gravel still shows the traces of recent tyre-marks. In the shade near the front door Liz is coming and going in English-looking sandals and a flowered dress. As Magali watches she emerges, carrying a plastic bowl, and empties it over a clump of wilting pink gladioli. As she turns to go inside again she looks up, squinting into the sunlight, and Magali draws back, away from the window. 'You told me they'd gone away!'

'I thought they had!'

He's so confident, it's unbelievable – lazing there on his elbows, his bare feet propped on the bale of hay. She says, 'That's the last time I take your word for anything!'

'Oh, come on! What does it matter? We had a great evening. How can you possibly say that?' He narrows his eyes at her and it's no good, she'd forgive him anything, she'd go anywhere with him if he asked her to. She remembers the two of them together in the dark pool and a shiver runs through her body. Is she really saying she wishes they'd stayed at home?

'No. I mean yes. It's okay, it's not your fault. They probably changed their plans. You couldn't be expected to know.' She tiptoes over to where she left her trainers and socks near the top of the ladder, and balances on one leg to put them on, brushing the sole of her foot against the fabric of her trousers to get rid of the hay. 'But we can't hang around. We need to be out of here. We just have to wait until her back's turned.'

Behind her he's putting his own things together. She hears the rasp and clink as he does up the buckles of his old backpack. 'Are you ready to go?'

She nods. Together they're standing at the head of the ladder. She nuzzles against him and he pulls her towards him, kissing the place where her hair starts just above her ear. She watches as he puts his foot on the top rung and feels below him for the next, disappearing step by step until only his head's left poking up above the level of the floorboards. Then his head goes too and he's reaching up towards her, his hand patting the top rung. 'Here.' She puts her foot where he's telling her. Then the next. In a moment she's standing beside him on the dirt floor of the barn.

They make their way along the side until they come to the wide arch with its apron of sunlight. Théo puts his head out for a second and draws it back. 'It's all right. She's not around. We'll make a run for it. Are you ready?'

She nods. But then she has a sudden thought. 'My backpack! I haven't got my things!'

He gestures towards the ladder. 'I'll go back for it.'

But it's worse than that. She's left it lying by the pool – the dirty underwear and T-shirt she rolled into a bundle when they took off their things and slipped into the water. Thank God she thought to keep her bank card in her pocket! When she tells him he volunteers to do a quick commando-style raid and rescue it, but she won't let him, it's too dangerous, it isn't worth the risk. Does he think she's going to let their whole future be ruined by a red-faced Englishwoman in a flowered dress? Forget it. She takes his hand and they run across the gravel and out behind the tall trees that grow along the side of the lane.

The bikes are exactly where they left them the night before, half concealed in the shade of the apple orchard. Théo pisses a long gold stream against a tree-trunk and she squats down quickly in the long grass. When she stands up he's already wheeled her bike out over the uneven ground to where the tarmac starts. He hands her his water bottle. 'We'll have to share this now.'

She takes a swig and wipes her mouth with the back of her hand. When she mounts the pedals the bike feels familiar, almost like a part of her own body. And without her ruck-sack she feels ridiculously light. She could be flying along, her wheels not even making contact with the ground. They reach the Champfleury junction and she goes to turn left, in the general direction of Toulouse.

But he stops her, his two feet on the ground and a hand on her handlebars so she can't move forward. She turns and looks at him. 'What's the matter?'

'Nothing. We're not going that way, that's all.'

She feels herself frowning. 'But you said . . .'

'It's not the same now. They'll know we've been here. They'll come looking for us in the van.'

'What, then?' Is he going to suggest they give it all up and just go back to Aubrillac, like nothing had happened?

'Don't worry.' He reaches across and caresses the back of her neck. 'We'll go a different way, that's all. Where they won't find us.' He stands on the pedals again and steers round towards the other road, the one that runs north-west. He turns to grin at her over his shoulder. 'Come on.'

She pulls back her own right pedal almost to the top of its arc and follows him more slowly. After a while she sees him stop and straddle the bike, waiting for her to catch up. She says, 'Where are we going?'

'Somewhere they won't think of looking for us.'

'Like?'

'You'll see.'

And after a while she does begin to see where they're heading. They cross the river and they're on the island of poplar plantations that stretches between the Taux and the man-made line of the canal. A little path leads down between the columns of trees. And then suddenly she understands what his plan is. And she's laughing again. She struggles to keep up with him, her bike's wobbling all over the place, she'll fall in if she isn't careful. And he's twisting on the saddle to look at her and laughing back. He's a genius! No one will even think of looking for them here. And now they're pedalling easily along the tow-path like they're on a Sunday afternoon outing, she's hardly even sweating, it's delicious, they're not making for Toulouse after all but somewhere totally different, the branches above them electric with crickets. She raises her head. Beside them, the milky greenish water of the canal; ahead, the raised white cockpit of a pleasure-cruiser moored at the next lock. On the opposite bank a rusty old pump belches away like an old toad. Over his right shoulder she can see a yellowish haze, as if a storm's coming. She brakes as the tow-path dips down under the shadow of a bridge. When they ride up the steep little slope on the other side the Jumelech towers loom towards them, nearer and nearer across the flat fields.

PETE

When the first drops started to darken the surface of the lane outside he was standing at the window, wondering if he could feel the pain coming again. But no, it was nothing. At least half the time it was all in his imagination. Life was too good here to let itself be spoiled by something so idiotic. The house – Seyrac, Champfleury, the whole setting – was so completely right. And the holiday lets were a piece of cake – it had all turned out to be far easier than he'd anticipated: hadn't they already got several very pleasant couples who'd booked in again for the same fortnight next year?

And Aubrillac itself was so French. He felt a surge of pride every time he showed it to someone new from England; it was as if this were his place now, as if the restoration of the covered marketplace, the archways and cobbled streets, the houses with their half-timbered pigeon-lofts, had been paid for by his own taxes, achieved with the sweat of his own brow. Whereas in fact it was all Jumelech conscience money, as everyone around here was only too happy to tell you. But all the same you had to admit it was extremely attractive – flowers everywhere, and the Sunday morning farmers' market spilling over with apricots and olives and pistachios and spit-roast chickens, little cheeses made from goats' and ewes' milk, and local honey. You only had to step into that deep shade and fill your arms with home-grown fruit and vegetables to realise this was a better kind of life, there was nowhere in England that could deliver anything even half as good.

It was starting to rain in earnest now. Better see to the pool. He went round the side of the barn and over to the rolled cover. He bent down to pick up the long guide-strap. And something caught his eye – something magenta and purple, lying on the paving to one side – it looked like a child's nylon rucksack, the kind little kids around here sometimes wore to school. He opened it and rummaged briefly inside – girls' clothes, a kid's book, one or two other things. He dropped it on the paving stones again while he finished unrolling the covers. By the time he'd snatched it up and run indoors the rain was sheeting down. His shirt was half-transparent, his shorts a shade darker. Water ran down his bare calves, soaking into his canvas shoes.

Inside, doors were banging. He ran from the front to the back of the house, closing windows. The rain billowed in white sheets, hitting the walls with such force that it seemed to make the whole building shake. Upstairs the drumming on the roof was deafening. One more gust like that and something would actually explode. And he'd forgotten the attic windows. Christ! He took the stairs two at a time but as he stuck his head above floor level a hailstone as big as a golf-ball came skittering across the boards towards him, stopping inches from his face. He retreated quickly, the lump of ice in his hand. In the kitchen he opened his fingers. The thing had an opaque, white centre surrounded by an outer layer that was as clear as glass. It was like a giant marble, or some alien creature's eye.

After a while the noise receded. Streams of water poured from the perforated gutters. It had gone so dark he couldn't see to read. He pressed a light switch but nothing happened. Somewhere in the direction of the cottages he thought he could hear someone crying. He pulled his old mac from a hook by the door and held it over his head as he went to see if everyone was all right.

In front of the end cottage there was a little huddle of bedraggled-looking people. An elderly woman was wailing something with her hand over her mouth – he couldn't make out the words. A plump girl in a short frilled skirt had her arm round her shoulders. She turned to him almost aggressively as he got near. 'My gran was with my dad in the car when the back window went. She freaked out – she thought we were being shot at.'

'I'm really sorry,' he said. 'We do have these storms occasionally. Are you all all right otherwise?'

'Except for the fucking car,' one of the men said.

Pete followed his eyes. Where the rear window had been there was a jagged rim of glass. Broken glass covered the back seat. The roof and bonnet were pitted with deep scars. Thank God he'd thought to put his own car away in the barn. He looked at the sky. 'It seems to have gone over anyway for the time being. They usually get the power back on within a few hours. But if you need anything, just give us a yell.'

Was that really all he could say to them? By his own door he stopped for a moment and listened. In the distance he could hear the muffled boom of the weather cannon, sounding about every eight seconds. Amazing, how they thought they could diffuse it – though why they hadn't tried a couple of hours ago he was at a loss to understand. The gravel around his feet was littered with broken-off branches and flower-heads and shards of plastic guttering. What on earth was Liz going to say when she came back?

He heard the car draw up as he was mopping the small flood that must have blown in under the kitchen door. She'd been at her embroidery club meeting, one of the few things she allowed herself to be persuaded to do on her own. A friend who was more confident about driving on French roads had picked her up and brought her back. He saw her grimace as she walked towards him. 'You've had a storm, I gather.'

'Didn't you?'

'No, nothing. Then, when we were driving back, the roads were suddenly wet and there were trees all over the place and I thought, Look out. And sure enough.' She lifted the head of a geranium in the pot by the door and broke it off in her fingers. 'Have you checked all the skylights?'

'Ours are all okay. No one in the cottages said anything, so I assume theirs are too. The attic room got a bit wet. I couldn't get to it in time.'

'Don't worry about it,' she said. 'It'll dry out.' She went past him into the kitchen and started filling the kettle.

'The power's off.'

'Oh. Yes, of course. It would be.' She put the kettle down and went over to check the freezer door was firmly closed.

He squeezed the water out of the mop and reached behind her to stand it in its usual place by the wall. 'You don't seem too upset. All your lovely flowers. I thought you might . . .'

'Oh . . .' She turned to look at the debris strewing the

gravel by the door. 'They'll grow back. That's the great thing about this place. Things go wrong – accidents happen – and it doesn't seem to matter. The next day the sun comes out and it's warm and everything's growing back. That's why I love it so much.'

He repeated stupidly, 'That's why you love it?'

She was giving him an odd look. 'What do you mean? Isn't that a good enough reason?'

He pulled out one of the chairs and sat down at the table. He rubbed his face with his hands. 'It's just . . . I thought you weren't all that happy here, that's all. I thought you were just going along with it because of me – because of how you knew I felt. Everything you do here seems so . . .'

'English?' She slid into the chair next to his. 'I suppose most of my friends *are* English. But that doesn't mean I don't want to be here. One or two of the people I've got to know lately happen to be French, actually. And I thought I'd sign up for some language classes in Aubrillac in the autumn. I got a B at O-level, did I ever tell you that?' Her eyes glinted in the light from the window. 'I've decided it's time I started reading French magazines and watching French TV.' Her hand was resting on the table. As she was speaking she'd closed it into a loose fist.

'Incredible,' he said.

She was looking at him. 'What?'

'I thought you were miserable here. I thought you were just waiting for the right moment to tell me. I just assumed you'd be only too glad for us to throw in our hand and go home.'

'But it's so beautiful!'

'What is?'

'Aubrillac. The market-place. The old houses down by the river. The church with those funny little towers. And that ridiculous bell that used to wake us up at seven every morning – we used to hear it even right out here in the sticks, don't you remember? And those lovely old carvings – the fish and birds with long beaks. Everything. I'd miss it all so much. Even the pilgrims. I know it's stupid. But I like the thought of them – all those odd bods trudging through with their boots and sticks and their enormous backpacks, all looking for something – Australians, Dutch, English, you name it. And French, of course.'

'And Jumelech?' He realised he was shivering. The temperature must have dropped a good five degrees since the storm hit.

'Oh well. I didn't expect you to understand.'

'I'm serious.'

She raised her eyebrows. 'Well, then, yes, if you really want to know. Even Jumelech. Gerry and I were driving through Aubrillac the other evening and there was this terrific sunset and if you'd been there you'd have reacted just the same, I know you would. Those two towers were . . . oh, I don't know . . . sort of strange and lovely in their own way. Everything ends up being beautiful in this place.'

That evening he had his work cut out. The storm had done more damage than he'd realised. The table-tennis table had blown over and wrapped one of its legs round an apple-tree. The cover of the pool was trailing in the water in several places, weighed down by drifts of melting hailstones. The whole patio area was ankle-deep in twigs and leaves and spiky green horse-chestnut cases like small grenades. One of the summer tenants had left a window unfastened and it had crashed open against the outside wall, shattering the glass. One of the others was anxious about the food in his refrigerator. One of the women wittered on endlessly about when she'd be able to do laundry and he told her he sincerely hoped it would be soon. By the end of the evening he was relieved to come in and find Liz had cleared away the dinner things and washed them by candlelight. His torch beam flicked over the neat shelves, the vase of flowers on the kitchen table, something purple and magenta slumped on the seat of one of the chairs.

He slipped off his sandals and padded into the bedroom, the leather heel-straps looped over one finger. He stood there for a moment, taking deep breaths in the stillness. After a while her sleepy voice came to him. 'Pete? What are you doing? Are you okay?'

And he wasn't, he realised. He really wasn't. While he'd been standing there listening to that insufferable woman the pain had been taking shape steadily, growing steadily nearer, twisting in his gut like a small flame. He could no longer pretend he couldn't feel it. He needed to sit down. He felt sick suddenly. He lowered himself on to the corner of the bed and waited for it to recede.

After a moment he said, 'Liz?'

Under the thin bedclothes she'd pulled herself half-upright. She lay propped on her elbows, the pale oval of her face turned to his. She said, 'You might as well tell me.'

He let out his breath in a long sigh. 'How–?'

'You don't have to be a genius. I know you. I've known for ages you were worrying about something. Is it money? Why don't you just tell me? It's hardly ever as bad as you think.'

He hesitated. She'd left the curtains open and he could see she was lying flat again, her face turned to the ceiling. He had a strong impulse to take her hand. Instead he said, 'It's not very good.'

'That crack in the cottage wall's getting wider, don't tell me. I knew we shouldn't have trusted that English surveyor. They're on to a nice little thing out here. They're probably all on the make.'

'It's nothing to do with the wall,' he said.

'What, then?'

'It's to do with me.'

'Tell me.' She slipped out from under the covers and knelt on the bed with her arms round him, her cheek next to his.

When he'd finished telling her she sat there in her flowered nightie for a long time without saying anything. He glanced at her to see how she was taking it. She was staring ahead of her, into the dark corner of the room. She was rubbing the side of her head, as if she'd found a bruise there. He could smell the coconut in her shampoo, the French almond hand-wash she used. And the smell of her own skin, that she'd brought with her from England. After a while he heard her swallow. She said, 'It may not be anything.'

He felt suddenly grateful. She hadn't said, 'I'm sure you're worrying unnecessarily' or even 'It's probably nothing'. She'd recognised the reality and what she'd given him was the truth – a gentle version of the truth. They both knew it could be something serious, and they both knew what they stood to lose. She wasn't about to empty it all of meaning by colluding in some elaborate fictional game. He took her hand across the crumpled sheet. 'You're right: it may not be.'

'And whatever it is . . .'

He waited for her to go on but she left the sentence unfinished. He couldn't keep the anxiety out of his voice as he said, 'Do you think we should go back?'

She turned her head towards him sharply. 'To England, you mean? Why on earth would we want to do that?'

He searched his mind for the best words. 'You don't . . . I mean . . . Do you think it might feel . . . ?'

She reached across and touched him on the shoulder. 'We'd be absolutely potty! You'll get much better treatment here. British hospitals can't hold a candle to the ones they have over here. You won't be kept waiting anything like as long.'

She was sitting up in bed now, leaning slightly towards him, the palms of her hands pressed flat against the mattress. He was reminded suddenly of the time, a few months ago, when the cover of the pool had slipped into the water and it had been too heavy for him to lift on his own, how together they'd wrestled with it for at least an hour, how she'd refused to give up, even when he'd decided it was a lost cause and gone in to leaf through the yellow pages. The day after, her hands had been blue with bruises. But they'd done it. They'd sat at the edge drinking a celebratory whisky as the sky went from red to slate blue to indigo and the last of the great oval puddles of water shrank steadily and finally drained away.

He said, 'I think for me it's just the language. I wasn't sure I'd be able to . . .'

She didn't laugh at him. She said, 'I'll just make you an appointment with that Doctor Perardi, the man who syringed my ear, remember? I got the impression he had loads of patients who're English. They all have. And we've got loads of people we can call on to help us if we need to. Jim MacLaren's new woman, Andrea, she speaks good French – she'll translate for us if necessary. Or Jean-Yves and Chloë.' He felt rather than saw her make a face. 'And we bought that big dictionary. It's about time it got a bit of use.'

The pain had gone now. He pulled her to him and let his hand slide up under her T-shirt, feeling her breasts and belly gently. She was amazing. He'd forgotten what she was like. And she was right – whatever it was, it was part of the experience of living here, part of the place, almost. The place itself would give them ways of coping. They might not be exactly identical to the ways they'd known back in England, but they'd be good and appropriate and as effective as they could be. For the time being anyway life went on. The moments of panic he'd had before he told her were a kind of solitary luxury: they didn't correspond at all to the measured reality of consultation and diagnosis and treatment, with Liz at his elbow quietly leafing through the pages for meanings.

She was still stroking his thin hair back from his forehead. She whispered something he didn't quite catch.

'What?'

'I said, in the autumn we can both do the language classes if you want. We'll get Marie-Jo to help us with the vocabulary. By Christmas we'll probably both be so good we'll be able to offer technical translation on the side.'

By the time the door woke him the power had come back on. He could see the red figures of the radio-alarm flashing next to his face. He struggled to hang on to the shreds of dream that were already slipping away.

He'd been sitting at a big open window that reminded

him of the french windows on to the garden at the back of the house he'd grown up in. Only outside, instead of the green lawn and the bird-bath and flower-beds he remembered, there was just a wall of bare earth, baked hard and cracking in the flat midday sunlight. As he watched, it went dark under the shadows of a flock of flying crows. Then a pair of crows flew in through the window and flapped up towards the ceiling, cawing in panic, surrounding him in a storm of black droppings, till they finally settled on a shelf above him, his whole body spattered with blotches of what looked like ink. He woke and listened for the pain but there was nothing. For a few moments he lay there, waiting for his heartbeat to return to normal. Beside him he could sense that Liz was awake too.

He felt her turn her head towards him on the pillow. He rolled over and threw an arm across where she lay. 'What was that?'

'Only Jack coming in.'

'What's the time?'

She craned her neck towards the radio-alarm on the bedside table, but the red figures were only flashing to show it needed to be re-set. He heard her feeling for her reading-glasses so she could peer at her wristwatch. 'Almost three.'

What on earth was he doing, staying out so late? Had he been with that girl all this time? 'I didn't hear his car.'

'You were asleep.'

'What's he playing at?'

'He's young.' She kissed the side of his neck. 'He's in love.'

Together they lay listening. The door of the refrigerator crashed open against the wall and thumped shut again. Something glugged and fizzed into a glass. Perrier. Then the rasp of the bread-knife. She sat up and swung her feet to the floor.

He put his hand on her arm.

'It's all right,' she said. 'I couldn't really get to sleep anyway.'

'I know.' He reached for his dressing-gown and pushed his arm into the inside-out sleeve. The silky material felt cold on his skin.

Jack was sitting at the kitchen table, reading last week's English language newspaper and eating bread and cheese. He grinned at them as they stood in the doorway blinking. 'Sorry. I didn't mean to wake you up.'

'Don't worry about it.' Pete yawned. 'I was in the desert, fighting off a flock of crows. You were doing me a favour.'

Jack raised his red eyebrows. He was so like Liz sometimes. He gestured to the bottle of water. 'Can I get you something?'

Liz said, 'Have you only just come back from Alex's? I hope you didn't wake up the whole village. Doesn't Susie mind?'

'She doesn't seem to.'

'Well . . .' Liz reached for a glass and poured herself some water. 'I'm not sure I'd be as relaxed as she is. In a little place like Champfleury . . . ?'

'May I?' Pete said. He sawed himself a hunk of bread and dug his knife into the cheese. He was suddenly ravenous. 'I shouldn't think they care all that much. You know what the French are like.'

'What are they like?' Liz asked him.

'About love? They think sex justifies everything, especially from the point of view of the male.'

Liz took a gulp of water. 'I'm not sure we should . . .' She spluttered and waved her hand in Jack's direction. Pete thumped her on the back gently until she found her voice again. 'How old did you say Alex was?'

'Eighteen.'

'Are you serious about her?'

'Tell me, are you two . . . ?'

They'd said it almost together. Jack was looking from one of them to the other, as if he didn't know who to reply to first. After a moment he stopped chewing and said, 'Have you both been . . . ?'

'Drinking?' Pete said. 'No.'

Jack was rolling a lump of bread between his thumb and middle finger. He put down the little grey ball and picked up another. 'I was just thinking I might stay here a bit longer, if you didn't have any objection.'

In the quiet of the kitchen the fridge hummed. Over Liz's head the clock ticked. He heard himself say, 'Didn't you have plans to go to Poland with your mates?'

'Tim's going somewhere else with his girlfriend now. And Matt's run out of money. But I meant . . .'

Liz said, 'Was it the third of October you said you had to be back?'

'Actually, I thought I might not go back. I thought it might be good to stay here – take a year out – if it's okay with you, that is. Then Alex and I can go on seeing each other.'

'Take a year out?' He could hear the tension in Liz's voice.

'Get a job. Live with you here for a bit. Unless you've got a problem with that.'

Pete screwed up his eyes and opened them again. He could feel them both looking in his direction, waiting for him to speak. But it wasn't that easy. Everything was changing so fast, and he needed to be honest. He pushed back his chair and went to the window. Was it beginning to get light? He could just make out the pool under its whitish, slightly grubby cover, the dark shapes of trees moving against a cloudy sky. That night they'd swum together, when Jack had made him turn the lights off, how other-worldly it had seemed. He'd been feeling old and worn out and worried about himself and Jack had just jumped in on him and laughed and he'd felt suddenly a lot better. How there'd been a sort of rightness in it – it was right that your kids should be young and bursting with energy when you were starting to feel old and anxious, right that they should outlive you: that was how things were meant to be. *Go for it*, was that what he'd said that night? And wasn't Jack showing he could do precisely that? And who was he anyway to tell him he was making the wrong decision? Could anyone know, in the end, how good or bad a decision it was? If it had been his own early career, and Liz . . . he'd have done well to go for Liz and let all that other stuff look after itself. Careers would always work themselves out, one way or the other – in the end you were bound to look back and see this vaguely linear pattern that led from childhood by a more or less circuitous route to eventual retirement and a time when you could finally live – when you *had* to live – fully in the present. But people weren't so predictable. And it was the people who mattered. You could always go back and have another shot at university, but you couldn't go back and meet the same person and make them love you over again.

When he turned round Jack had gone. Liz gestured to him with her head and eyes. He went over to her and stood stroking her hair gently. 'I suppose he's got to do it,' he said. 'And we've got to let him. He'll find out eventually what he really wants.'

'But . . .'

He leaned over and kissed her upside-down on the fore-head. 'Don't worry. If it lasts it lasts. And if it doesn't . . .'

'He'll soon get the message.'

He stood behind her, his arms loosely crossed round her neck, the two of them swaying slightly, his eyes closed. 'It worked for us.'

'Mm.' She sighed, and he felt the warmth of her breath. 'What's that?'

'What?'

'That thing on the chair.' He made an effort to focus. She was pointing at the little rucksack. 'Where did it come from?'

'It's nothing. I found it by the side of the pool when I got back from Aubrillac the other morning. I haven't a clue who it belongs to. Some kid, presumably. I thought one of us could take it into the Champfleury post office and give it to that old geezer, the one who used to be the schoolteacher – he'll probably know.'

She nodded vaguely. She said, 'He always seems to know everyone. He probably knows the name of every pilgrim passing through.'

JULIEN

Why the devil had Pierre got it into his head that they should meet here and not at the Platanes as usual? An over-priced, pretentious place it always had been, full of American tourists and Parisians with too much money for their own good. And yet. It had its charm, there was no denying the fact. Sitting here on the terrace with the light dappling the white linen tablecloths, you could almost imagine you were in a different country, on holiday. And how many years was it since he'd had a holiday? Seven or eight – it was when he last went up to Castillon and visited the tower. And what an experience that was. Just thinking of the place made him feel suddenly almost faint – all those wonderful sixteenth-century books and manuscripts. And Michel had been brought up to speak Latin, imagine! What could possibly make you more aware of who you were than to be a solitary child speaking that marvellously lucid language, when everyone around you was blathering about the weather and the price of duck's liver in peasant French?

'Monsieur?' The street opposite came back into focus. Someone was standing at his elbow, trying to get his attention. He recognised Nathalie Fayard, in a short black dress with a little white pinny, a jotting pad and pencil in her hand.

'I'm waiting for someone. We'll give you our order when he arrives.'

She nodded at him and turned away, cocking her little pencil at another table, her head on one side. He wished she'd take that stupid grin off her face. None of those Fayards was ever very bright. He crossed and uncrossed his legs under the table. That was better. What could Pierre have meant by settling on this place? Was the Platanes suddenly not good enough? He looked up at the clock tower but from here the angle was too oblique, the face was unreadable. His own watch said six minutes to. And here was that silly girl back again, buzzing round him with a complimentary apéritif and a plate of little crusts spread with something dark and lumpy-looking. It wasn't even as if he were intending to stay. If he didn't drink anything much and went to bed early he might just manage to break the pattern: for once sleep would come quickly and spirit him off in less time than it took to say it, before he could start counting a single sheep.

'Monsieur? Is something the matter?' The girl was still hovering over him like an idiot. 'Isn't the Brulhois cold enough?'

'It's perfectly nice, thank you, Nathalie.' *Go back to your desk and sit down*, he almost said. Without realising what he was doing he was waving her away. What must she think of him? But they didn't bear grudges, that family. She was a good girl. He looked over towards the corner under the awning and saw her eyes shining. He pulled his face into a smile.

What did she think of him? He was losing touch. For a moment the green blinds of the little Casino supermarket opposite blurred and he shut his eyes. Even now, he asked nothing more than to be allowed to sleep. It was such a simple thing. His whole soul was turning to cardboard and he was powerless to stop it. They could fold him in on himself like a box, first the flaps on the ends, then the longer flaps along either side and then if they put their whole weight on it the whole thing would collapse inwards and the air that was his soul would wheeze its way out and never reach its destination, no one would even be able to read the address . . .

'Having a little nap, old man?' He looked up and saw Pierre standing over him, his eyes crinkled up with concern. 'Listen, you can't do this to me. Not tonight. We were going to have the gastronomic. It isn't every day, l'Horloge. Are you going to fall asleep with your head in the soup?'

'I thought you didn't estimate l'Horloge very highly?' he said.

'That's just sour grapes. I can't afford to like it very often.'

He laughed in spite of himself. 'Is that what it is. And what's happened to inspire this sudden extravagance, might I ask? Have you come into some money, or are we here to celebrate?'

Pierre looked round, tipping his head slightly sideways and raising an eyebrow in a way Julien had never managed to imitate. 'So. What are you going to have?' Nathalie was at their table at once, placing an open menu in Julien's hand with a barely detectable flourish. His eyes ran down the list of rich dishes. *Foie gras, gambas, magret, tarte aux abricots* . . . could he possibly eat all that? He had a sudden yearning for something really simple – Eliane's lettuce salad, perhaps, or a slice of one of her home-grown melons. He hadn't the stomach any more for all this rich stuff. 'What's all this in aid of?' he said.

Pierre picked up his fork and twisted it so the prongs

caught the last of the sunlight. 'Are you sleeping any better these days?'

'Not really.'

'Have you asked the doctor to give you something?'

He hesitated. 'I've got my own doctor.'

Pierre raised his eyebrows again.

'Le Seigneur de Montaigne.' He shifted his position slightly, knocking against the table. His glass of Brulhois shivered, not yet touched.

Pierre leaned back in his chair, half-smiling. 'Ah.'

'He has a wise word for everything.'

'So you keep telling me.'

'Seriously. He does.'

'So what does he have to say about insomnia?' Pierre raised his glass and leaned across the white tablecloth to clink it against Julien's own. 'Tell me. What gems does he have for us there?'

' "Life is a dream." '

'Is that all?' Pierre gave a short laugh. 'Well, I'll drink to that. I'll repeat that to myself every morning and think of you as I get out of bed.'

Julien opened his mouth and closed it again. He'd been going to give him the rest of the quotation, but it was casting pearls before swine, obviously. Instead something made him say, ' "Unless a man feels he has a very good memory, he should never venture to lie." '

Pierre was frowning. 'That's not about sleep, is it?'

'It's about honesty,' Julien said. The girl was at their shoulders with her little pad and pencil. He wanted to say, 'Not now, Nathalie.' Instead they gave her their order and she tripped away.

'Right,' Pierre said. He tapped out a cigarette and sat with his head lowered and his arm stretched across the table, a ribbon of smoke rising between the leaves. 'As you like.' Above their heads the trees were strung with fairy-lights, the dark flex threaded in and out between the branches. Pierre was rolling the tip of his cigarette against the side of the ashtray, trimming the ash to a point. 'I'm leaving Aubrillac. I've decided to sell up and go and live with my daughter. Nicole.'

It was as if someone had punched him in the chest. 'You're leaving?'

'They've bought a house that's big enough for me to have my own bedroom and bathroom and a little kitchen. You'll be able to come and visit.' He coughed. 'You've got to be realistic, old man. We're not going to get any younger.'

' "One must always have one's boots on and be ready to go." '

'Precisely.'

Through the arch of the clock-tower he could hear the shouts of children playing in the square. Suddenly he could hardly keep his eyes open. Then Nathalie Fayard came with the entrées, and the smell of the duck pâté filled his nostrils. He began to feel slightly better again.

Perhaps if you really concentrated you could make it go away. If, when you started to feel the panic building, you blocked it from your thoughts, making your mind a smooth, blank surface despair had no hold on – if you just lay there and forced yourself to breathe deeply and think only in, out, in, until the thing went away. The attacks were short – a few seconds, a minute at most. If he could just hold on and resist it, eventually it would get fed up with him and leave him alone.

But it was making him crazy. When he looked in the bedroom mirror what he saw was a grey-faced old man on the way out, almost a corpse. This was how he'd look in his coffin. You didn't need the slightest spark of imagination to be able to visualise exactly how it would be. And Pierre was leaving. What was he going to do? Who would he talk to now in the café on summer evenings? Who would he share books with in the winter? *In solitude, be a world unto yourself*. It was all very well for old Michel to say it, but he wasn't sure he had enough in his self now to make a world out of. He needed someone to care about him, someone to ask him if he was getting any sleep. Now he'd be on his own – except for Eliane. He sniffed. Well, she could always be counted on to look after him with words of comfort and elbow-grease. She was as good as a wife to him. If he threw his shirt on the floor she'd pick it up. A few days later it would be back in the pile on the end of his bed, washed and ironed, folded as neatly as it had been the day it was new.

He got undressed, almost losing his balance as he stepped out of his trousers, steadying himself with a hand on the back of the chair. He'd have done better to stick to three glasses, but it had been hard to resist. The food at l'Horloge wasn't bad, you had to admit it. You had to have the odd glass or two to do it justice. And Pierre had been in the mood to push the boat out, obviously, to mark the occasion. The occasion of leaving him here alone in this godforsaken little *bled* to rot.

He dozed off almost immediately, the wine sending him into a heavy, almost dreamless sleep, and woke to hear a clock striking three in the distance, his mouth dry as sand, his throat aching. He must have been snoring. It was those commercial wines – not like the local stuff you bought in a jug straight from the barrel. The sulphites played havoc with the system. He'd have a headache when he woke up in the morning, probably. If he ever got to sleep again, that was. And if he ever woke up.

A faint line of light shone on the ceiling, cast by the crack above the curtains. He lay looking up at it and let his eyes go out of focus. He could feel his eyelids starting to close. He was falling, falling . . . And crack, he was awake again. And somewhere at the end of a dark tunnel a little twist of something was growing towards him, pushing at the edges of his mind, pulsing with his heartbeat as it pressed against his sleepy consciousness and tried to pour itself into him through the cracks. No. He covered his mind tightly and the thing rippled over the surface like dry ice, trying to find a way in. But he wasn't going to let it. He knew all its names – pain, despair, failure, death – and he knew what it did to him. He turned over and shrugged the sheet up over his shoulder, burying his face in the pillow. And a moment later he was falling asleep again.

He was at Jumelech with a class of children: it was a school trip. He counted the heads as they rushed ahead of him into the entrance to the fish-ladder: Nathalie Fayard, wearing a little white apron and sucking her thumb, Martin and Magali Verge, Antoine du Boucher, swinging a string bag of marbles. Olivier Simon in a world of his own as usual, running his fingers absent-mindedly along the walls. Catherine Morand scowling. And his own brother Marcel, looking younger and healthier than he had for years. All present and correct. They lined up on either side of him, pressing their faces flat against the murky glass. 'Do you see?' he was saying to them. 'When they built the plant they had to re-route the water so they could use it for cooling. But they built this 'staircase' so the fish could swim up or down and find the water again at the other end. Do you see?'

All around him they were nodding their heads gravely. Marcel reached out and took his arm. 'They're going to be okay,' he said. For a moment their eyes met.

The children squinted at the greenish glass, trying to see something. A shoal of little bright blue fish swam into view and darted backwards and forwards, trying to find the way through. And then something seemed to be not quite right. There was an odd kind of orange glow over everything. All round him he heard the words 'Red Alert' rising in a whisper, echoed from one child to the next. It didn't surprise him. He'd been expecting it, even. It was those English people's fault: it was because of the London bombings. They'd brought the Al Qaeda threat here with them, it was like a contagion, that fatuous Tony Blair and his opportunistic decision to support Bush over Iraq . . .

The orange light intensified. And then out of the murk a huge face swam towards them, nosing the glass – a huge dogfish face with trailing whiskers and half-open mouth, its grey skin speckled and flaking with what seemed to be some terrible disease. And suddenly he found he was weeping. The children around him were all dying – even little Nathalie, even Olivier and Catherine, damn her – even his brother Marcel with the strong, warm grip and gentle eyes. He woke to find his own eyes were wet. He was actually crying. He felt a warm weight on his left arm – Chéri was curled in a soft ball in the crook of his elbow. He put out his other hand and stroked gently, letting the tears slowly dry on his skin. After a while Chéri started to purr, the little body vibrating with pleasure under his fingers.

He went into the kitchen and turned on the light. The clock above the stove said just after three o'clock. He shivered. It was cool since the storm, almost cold. He picked up his old cotton sweater from the back of a chair and shrugged it on over his pyjamas. He went to close the window. Outside it was raining, he could hear it swishing gently on the leaves of the cherry tree, making a soft gurgle as it ran down into the earth. He reached across the table for the book that was lying face downwards on the formica – that story about the Jewish boy and the marbles, what was that doing here? And then he remembered – it had been in that child's backpack the red-headed English boy had given him yesterday morning. What was he supposed to do with it? He was damned if he could remember now.

He sat and listened to the rain falling. So Pierre was leaving Aubrillac. Well, he was just going to have to get used to it. They'd visit each other sometimes, perhaps: Dijon wasn't as far away as it might have been – not as far as Lille, say, or Le Havre. And they would both surely write. He might even try using the post office computer to get some sort of conversation going by what they liked to call 'Mail'. He wrinkled his face in distaste. 'Courriel' was a better word. It was friendlier, more natural, less arrogant. When he started composing his first missives to Pierre he'd have to think of it as that.

He went into the bedroom for his Montaigne. As if by instinct, his hands found the essay on friendship and he began to read. Such a comprehensive man, le Seigneur de Montaigne. So truthful, to admit his great love for his dead

friend, La Boëtie. There was a kind of generosity here, a large-
ness of spirit that transcended ordinary friendship and loss.
He read on, until he reached the one quotation that every
schoolchild in France knew – the reason behind that great
male love: 'Because he was who he was, because I was me.'
You couldn't get more personal than that. Or more univer-
sal. Generation after generation of French men and women
had allowed themselves to be touched by it, for the past four
hundred years. He lifted his head and sat gazing into space,
his eyes unfocused. The rectangle of sky at the window had
lightened slightly. Was the rain stopping or was dawn finally
on its way?

He read on further. Gradually the new day *was* beginning: every time he looked up at the end of a paragraph the
sky above the cherry tree was slightly paler. The branches
themselves were beginning to emerge and stretch, the leaves
opening, twisting towards the light. Somewhere over to his
left a bird twittered. He waited for another one to answer it
but there was nothing. *You must have been mistaken, little bird – it's
still too early.* But the sound came again, clear and confident as
before. And this time there was an answering chirrup, from
somewhere quite close at hand.

He closed the book and pushed back his chair. His legs felt
stiff, his knees twingeing and cracking as he stood up and put
his weight on them to hobble to the window. God, he really
was getting old! A few more years and they'd be nagging
him to take one of those walking-frame things, they'd be
coming to bolt hand-rails on to the walls in his bathroom,
there wouldn't be any part of his life he could call his own.
But it was nonsense. He leaned out across the sill and breathed
the smell of the grass after rain, a rush of wet earth and leaves

and flowers, laced with a faint whiff of diesel from the Arnot kid's motorbike, blown here from across the corner of the field. He still had all his faculties, he was still able-bodied. He was certainly good for another few years yet. And so what if he felt wrong-footed by Pierre's news? Didn't loss betoken richness? *Because he was who he was. Because I was me.* He'd been incredibly lucky. And Pierre had been lucky too. He closed his eyes for a moment and saw Pierre's face as it had been that evening – quizzical, half-ironic, yet somehow, under it all, pained. It couldn't have been easy for him either. He'd decided to leave his life here behind, that it was the only thing he *could* do in the circumstances: he had to be reasonable and listen to his daughter's urgings and look ahead. But he was sorry. For all Julien knew, he was lying awake himself, staring up at the ceiling, wondering if he'd made the right decision. In their separate lives, the two of them were lonely together. There was a kind of sad comfort in that.

All the birds were singing now. From over in the direction of Aubrillac he heard a clock strike six. He could make out each leaf of the cherry, an intricate black silhouette against the grey-blue of the clouds. And just where the far hedge met sky, a rim of orange. It was almost daylight. He walked over to the door and switched off the fluorescent tube. For a moment the kitchen went black. And then little by little he began to make out the shapes and colours – the pale formica of the table, a saucepan gleaming on the wall, the lumpy shape of the little rucksack on the seat of a chair, its purple straps and magenta panels coming to life as he watched.

What was he supposed to do with it? He rubbed his eyes, seeing the boy's freckled face again. The kid's French hadn't been that good, and his own English was non-existent now.

It's all right, he'd wanted to tell him. Start again and take it slowly. I'm listening. But the young man had just gabbled something at him and run off before he could take it in properly, leaving the bag in his hands.

Eliane would know. She knew everyone in the village; she was his private news service sometimes, filling him in on who'd got a mistress hidden away in Toulouse and who'd had to go to the doctor's to get their varicose veins looked at and who'd had a small win on the lottery, which children were taking their First Communion and when. Pity it was her day off. But as soon as he'd finished his morning session in the post office he'd go over and find her and ask. She'd probably make a bit of a fuss of him. If he timed it right she might even ask him to stay to lunch.

He hadn't quite bargained with how strong the sun was. By midday the rain had cleared completely and everything glittered. The plume of steam from the right-hand Jumelech tower had shrunk to a barely visible puff. He'd forgotten to bring his hat. As he walked he mopped his perspiring forehead with his handkerchief. The surface of the road had dried already and the corners of his eyes prickled with dust. This not-sleeping business couldn't go on. He'd have to go to the doctor and get something. He wasn't a bad sort, Perardi, with his shock of wiry hair and that Corsican accent you could cut with a knife. He did put his pen down and sit back in his chair and listen if you tried to tell him something. He didn't actually laugh in your face or make you feel you were an old fool. And it wasn't such a terrible admission. No one could be expected to go on like this for ever without some kind of help.

The three kilometres to Eliane's house seemed much longer than he remembered. He trudged along the straight road between corn and sunflowers, the big seed-heads already blackened and shrivelling, unrecognisable. It was a relief to get to the avenue of planes and walk from shadow to shadow. He was reminded of how he used to carry messages sometimes as a teenager, running up the edges of orchards and through the woods, or down along the dark banks of the river, never even stopping, it seemed to him now, to get his breath.

He stopped and mopped his head again. The sweat was making his eyes sting. Under the little backpack his shirt was soaked. He took the straps from his shoulders for a moment and carried it in his hand, feeling the wet cloth between his shoulder-blades get slowly warmer as it dried in the sun. Perhaps he was foolish even to have attempted this? Perhaps he was exposing himself to some hidden danger – a heart attack, a stroke even? A sunburnt head, at the very least. *What were you playing at, old man? Do you want them to think you've got Altzheimer's?* In his mind he heard Pierre's voice and found himself smiling. *It was your fault, you old rogue. You were the one who stopped me sleeping last night. And I'm old enough now to do as I bloody well like. Because I'm me.*

He'd reached Eliane's turning at last. He recognised the ramshackle farm buildings on the corner of the lane. He mopped his face and neck one last time and shoved the ball of wet handkerchief right down inside his pocket. He didn't want her to think there was anything wrong.

But as he approached the house he could hear voices. Was she talking to a neighbour? But no: when he got closer he could see there was a big table set up in the shade at the side of the house, with what looked like a large family group clustered round it eating and drinking. Small children stumbled about with carts or rode tricycles under the trees. Who were all these people? There were old faces – some of them surely older than his own – and young ones. He realised with a shock that he'd never been the slightest bit curious about her life, that in spite of what she'd undoubtedly told him, he'd always somehow thought of her as coming from the same sort of family as he did, always somehow visualised her as essentially alone.

She came to meet him, smiling, and kissed him on both cheeks, putting her hand through his arm and gently pulling him forward. 'You've never met my family. My parents, my sister and her husband, my elder brother, my cousin Jean-Yves . . .' There were so many of them. He'd really had no idea! And here he was standing there like an old fool, blinking. 'We've just got to the dessert. You'll stay and have a piece of tart and a digestif with us?'

But he couldn't possibly. He felt himself colouring and starting to sweat again. He put the little rucksack into her hands.

She listened gravely as he stumbled over the story. 'Who did you say brought it?'

He told her again.

'Well then, it's obvious. It must be the young girl's – the one who works for that Mme MacLaren with the baby – the two of them have been going round together for weeks now, you see them all the time. Don't you worry about it. Come and sit in the shade for a bit, have a rest. Jean-Yves'll run you back in a minute, and he'll drop it in to her – Champfleury's more or less on his way.'

He handed her the rucksack, shaking his head. He felt suddenly shy. With her cheeks flushed pink from the food and wine she struck him as almost pretty. She was watching him, her eyes crinkled up with what seemed to be amusement. He hung his head, half tongue-tied. 'Thank you. You're very kind. But I won't stay.' As he turned to make his way back down the lane towards home the voices and laughter came after him.

ALEX

Who would have thought it would all turn out to be this amazing? She thinks of her friends back in England, how they'd laugh at her for not minding being stuck out in the sticks all summer, for liking it, even – so much that now she's actually begging to be allowed to stay on. At home they'll all be hanging round the precinct, sitting with their arms and legs draped over the arms of the benches, waving cigarettes and drink-cans and squealing with laughter. She can see them staggering home at night with their arms round one another's shoulders, dizzy with spliffs and beer. But it's weird, she's actually happy here. She lifts Jade out of the pushchair and sets her in the baby swing, settling the safety-bar over her little fat thighs. She gives her a gentle shove and the swing starts to sway backwards and forwards. Every time it comes to meet her she says, 'Bo!', and every time she says it Jade lets out the same throaty chortle. Over her shoulder the sun's getting lower, their two shadows stretching across the grass. Somewhere over to her left the clock strikes seven, seven. How funny she used to think that was, when she first arrived in the village – the way it struck every hour and waited a few seconds and then struck the same hour again.

She couldn't imagine ever getting used to it. And now it's like the most natural thing in the world.

And this is what happiness feels like. Jack . . . The low trees behind the playground go fuzzy round the edges and she blinks them clear again. And all that stuff with Jason seems like it happened centuries ago, it might have been another life. Her friends' relationships are so childish, really – how can she ever go back to all that? How can she just go back and live in her parents' cramped house like she's still a little girl? If she turns her head she can see woods and fields spreading out into the distance for miles and miles. Just her and Jack and the swing ticking backwards and forwards across the grass, and Jade laughing. There's nowhere she wants to be at this moment so much as here.

She's waiting for the swing to die down when a car draws up at the edge of the green. She sees Susie leaning out of the open window. 'Alex?'

'Yeah?' She leaves Jade swinging and goes over.

'Look, it's getting a bit late, and I've got to go – I'm supposed to be over at Laura's at half past. Just give Jade her supper, can you? Don't worry about her bath if you're tired – I'll do it in the morning. Have a good evening, both of you. Oh, and . . .' She gropes for something in the back of the car. 'Someone just dropped this in for you. It's from Jack.'

'Thanks.' She opens her hands for what seems to be a bundle of cloth. It's a child's purple and magenta rucksack, its plastic buckles straining. She stands holding it in her outstretched arms like an idiot. What is it? And what's he doing sending it to her like this, rather than just bringing it over himself? Is it some kind of present? The car pulls away, narrowly missing a rock that someone's left lying in the road.

She bends to pick it up and put it back in the pile with the others. Behind her Jade's swing has come almost to a standstill. She lowers herself on to the tyre next to it and pushes backwards, her toes digging into the dirt. In a moment she'll launch herself into the air.

But she lets the swing come back to the vertical. She reaches across and sets the other one in ragged motion again, making Jade squeal and wave her arms. Then she slides the plastic buckles of the rucksack open with two little clicks and loosens the toggle on the drawstring to reach inside.

It's a book, she can feel the corners. She pulls it out, turning it over to scan the blurb. It's some wartime story, something about a boy escaping. *Why is he sending me this?* Then something soft – a T-shirt, black, with some pseudo-Japanese logo – cool, though it doesn't look brand new. Did it just catch his eye at the market or what? And then something small and hard – a roll-on deodorant – and what the fuck's this? A toilet glove and a little piece of soap that leaves its cold and slime all over her fingers. Yuk. And someone else's toothbrush and battered-looking tube of toothpaste, held together by a rubber band. She doesn't get it. Is it some kind of joke? Is there something he's trying to tell her? Is it a kind of code – is it his way of saying, 'Come away with me' or what?

She's almost at the bottom now. Her fingertips brush against something silky. She tugs and out it comes – a small bundle of women's underwear – a bra and several pairs of knickers, one of them crumpled into a tight ball. She almost laughs aloud with the surprise. What—? She feels suddenly cold. The ropes of the swing pull tight against her, squeezing her upper arms. For a moment she's back in the throbbing dark of Casa Mia, and the dance-floor's tilting upwards towards her face. Her throat's suddenly dry, her hands are shaking. Why on earth would he want to send her a bag stuffed with some other girl's underwear? What can he possibly be trying to say?

She closes her eyes and sees darkness. Like with Jason that night. She can smell the smoke, feel herself running down a dark passage, feel her bare arms brushing the condensation on the walls. *How could he?* On that manky old sofa in the alcove with that slag Charlotte Reynolds? The two of them wide-eyed and staring, his hand still up under her skirt. Charlotte's face sort of glittery, like she was wearing fancy dress. *Sorry, sorry, sorry,* was that what he'd said afterwards? But it *wasn't enough.* If you really cared about someone it wasn't enough to apologise *after* you'd done something like that. If you really cared you wouldn't want to hurt them in the first place. He was pathetic. His apologies were pathetic. They didn't even begin to explain. All they did was salve his own conscience, let him pretend he didn't have to take any responsibility for anything he did. He was a coward. He was too scared to tell her to her face. So he sent her some coded message and left her on her own to puzzle it out while he was free to feel completely innocent, free to go on to the next thing.

She feels sick. Slowly she stuffs the things back into the little magenta and purple bag. She lifts Jade from the swing to the pushchair and starts to wheel it across the grass. Should she get rid of the thing somehow? But maybe it isn't what she's thinking, perhaps she's got it wrong? She has to confront Jack with it at least, give him the chance to explain himself. It might not mean what she thinks it means. She just has to see him – quickly. Tonight. In the shadow of the shelter she crouches by the buggy and feels the tears starting to well up, her nose suddenly streaming. She pulls out a crumpled tissue and wipes her face. She buries her head for a moment in her arms. *Make it go away. Make things what they were before. Make time go backwards.* She takes a deep breath, forcing herself to concentrate on the little noises – a cricket somewhere in the grass, birds twittering in the trees. The grass-blades tickling her bare ankles. She feels Jade move in the buggy next to her, touching her hair, patting her head gently like she's a passing village cat.

She wheels the pushchair slowly back, lowering her head and stopping to wipe her cheeks with the tissue whenever the tears come. In Susie's kitchen she lifts Jade out, hugging the solid little body for a moment against her own. There's a murmur of voices from the next door garden and a wisp of blue smoke hanging over the newly clipped hedge – so the old Pirottets are getting ready to have a barbecue – trust them to choose the best possible moment! She goes over and closes the glass door to the garden. No point filling the whole house with their disgusting smells.

She hates them. She hates the way they're always out there fiddling about with something – dribbling over their plants with the hose or worrying at the privet or gossiping to one of the neighbours. Or sounding off in loud voices to their stupid dog. They're so typical of this whole dead-and-alive place. Is it possible that less than an hour ago she was half-wishing she could stay in this shithole for the rest of her life?

She almost laughs. There she was, wishing she could stay here with him and all the time he was probably already messing about with someone else. And it wasn't just a spur-of-the-moment thing, either. If you weren't actually plan-ning to sleep with someone why would you pack a bag? She winces. But through the pain of it she feels something else – like this is what she's been expecting, like ever since that night in Casa Mia she's always known it was going to happen again. It's almost a kind of relief. At least he did find a way of telling her, however devious. At least he isn't going to let her go on loving him. He isn't going to sit back and wait for her to find out the truth. It's not like he's going to do what Jason did, letting her follow him all over for days till she finally caught up with him and Charlotte Reynolds that night in Casa Mia in the ear-splitting dark.

She hates him though. She hates everyone. She'll take the little rucksack up to Seyrac and confront him with it, see what he has to say for himself, make him tell her the whole thing. Maybe – just maybe – it isn't as bad as she's letting herself imagine. Even though part of her already knows.

She's not hungry. When she's fed Jade and put her down in her cot she pours herself a glass of rosé from the open bottle in the door of Susie's fridge and takes it out into the garden. The barbecue's died down now: in the sky above the privet hedge she can see just the faintest shimmer. You can hardly even tell it's there. She pulls out the old deckchair that's leaning by the door and puts it up. Shit. She's forgotten to bring in the washing. All Jade's things will stink of smoke and firelighters and scorching fat. But who cares? She lets her head fall back on the canvas and watches the little shadowy limbs waving gently to and fro above her against a background of stars.

When Susie comes back Alex doesn't say anything. She slips back to her own flat to pull on her jeans and trainers and then goes out, with the backpack slung over one shoulder.

She hasn't thought to bring a torch, but she can see enough anyway. The playground's deserted now, the swings like some sort of scaffold, the window of the pilgrim shelter a patch of lurid yellow against the black. As she goes past it she sees someone moving, the shape of a head coming and going inside. Unrolling his sleeping-bag on one of the slatted wooden seats, probably. She thinks of him eating and sleeping there in that tiny space, using the dank toilet with weeds growing out of the cracks in the walls, washing himself at the cold tap. And tomorrow, shrugging on the straps of his backpack and going on.

Her eyes are beginning to adjust to the light now. She can see the tiny flints gleaming at the edge of the road, and the pale heads of the hydrangeas in front of the cottages at the corner. As she passes the old village school she can read the numbers still painted on the walls. She can make out the name 'Champfleury', crossed through with a red line. She takes the main road, towards Seyrac, and walks steadily along the gravelly verge. She's got the little rucksack on her back now – she could be some kind of night hiker herself – or a pilgrim choosing to clock up the miles while it's cool instead of in the heat of the day.

She walks downhill towards the Seyrac turning, just before the valley levels out into the broad flood plain of the river, meandering towards the town. A motor-bike whizzes past her, so close she gives a little scream. Above the big trees on the bend the sky looks pale, as if it's near dawn already. Then an edge of something white pushes itself up from behind them, like a paper petal of French confetti – the moon. She thinks suddenly of a wedding she saw a couple of weeks ago in Aubrillac, that idiotic photographer arranging the couple like dolls in unnatural poses for what must have been more than an hour while he leaped about like a gnome, pointing his various pieces of equipment in their faces. The bride and groom looked almost shame-faced. And then all those ribboned cars charging through, rattling over the cobbles, honking and honking, like they were all exasperated, stuck in some endless traffic-jam. When the dark car swerves and pulls up a few paces ahead of her her first impulse is to turn round and start running uphill in the opposite direction. Then someone winds down a window and she recognises Damien.

His grinning face looks odd in the moonlight – all sharp shadows, like something out of one of the old black and white films her gran used to watch sometimes on TV. He seems suddenly about twenty years older. 'Where are you going, alone, so late in the evening? Do you want to come in the car?'

The words are harmless enough, but she shakes her head. 'Thanks. I'm only going to Seyrac. It's not worth driving.'

'I can take you. You don't want to walk on a road alone at night. With the car you'll arrive in five minutes.' He leans across and opens the passenger door for her.

She feels tears pricking her eyes again and blinks them back. He's right: this isn't really any fun at all. And the sooner she can get to Jack the sooner she'll know for certain. 'Okay then. Thanks.' She slips the straps of the rucksack from her shoulders and slides in beside him, holding it in her lap.

In front of them the road's lit up by his headlights, the shadows between tree-trunks are paths leading off to God knows where. He turns his head towards her and grins again. 'I told you I will take you for a drive. Now you can speak French.'

For the first time this evening she finds herself smiling.

It's an odd sort of smile, like she's holding the corners of her mouth up with her fingers. 'Seyrac's only a couple of miles,' she says. 'We won't have time.' But he shrugs and turns his head to grin at her and doesn't slow down. Already they're past the turning. She swivels in her seat and sees the finger-post shrinking in the back window. 'You've missed it,' she tells him. 'You'll have to take a left and go back.'

He doesn't answer. He feels in the glove compartment for his cigarettes and shakes one out, his hands still half-resting on the wheel. She tenses and fixes her eyes on the road ahead, hearing the click of the lighter. When he exhales she can smell the alcohol on his breath. God! He shouldn't be driving! She leans forward in her seat, watching the side of the road for an opening where they can draw in and turn.

'Slow down. You're going too fast.'

'Why?' He glances sideways at her and laughs. 'You are so careful, you English. You are all afraid of something. You never really notice you are moving at all.'

'But you can't see where to stop.' She hears her voice rising in a kind of squeak. 'We've got to find somewhere to turn round.'

'Why turn round?'

'You're driving me to Seyrac, remember? That was the Seyrac road we passed a couple of minutes ago.'

'We will go to Seyrac after,' he says easily.

They're bowling along a straight, flat road beside a row of poplars, the trees casting long shadows across the tarmac in the moonlight. It's like the two of them are tangled inside the spokes of a giant wheel. Her voice comes out as a sort of croak. 'Où allons-nous?'

'Mirlac. I told you. To the Truite d'Or. We can swim.'

'At this time of night? Are you completely crazy?'

His face pretends to be offended. He's not so frightening really. He's just clowning about, he's like an overgrown kid. 'Why crazy? The Truite d'Or will be closed but the place is beautiful. You'll see.'

Out of the corner of her eye she can see the door-handle gleaming next to her right elbow. No good trying to get him to turn round now, obviously. Seyrac's a long way behind them already. Something makes her say, 'I was going to see my boyfriend.'

'Ah . . .' He's doing that French thing with his mouth, a sort of pout. 'The English boyfriend. He is so young. And you are a woman with a woman's feelings. You need someone more . . .'

'More like you?' My God! What has she just said? He won't realise she was being sarcastic.

'Precisely.' He lifts his hand from the wheel to tap ash off his cigarette. A flake of something hot blows back in through the open window and lands on her arm. She jumps and brushes it off. He says, 'Someone to . . . wake you up. Someone who can show you what love is. Someone who is more a man.' He lifts his hand to his face again and the tip of the cigarette glows red.

A man! She hardly dares open her mouth. She watches the moon travel with the car. As they turn a corner it swims out above the trees into a patch of clear sky. The road's starting to climb. *I don't want a man ever again. I don't want anyone.* But there's something slightly pathetic about Damien somehow, and she doesn't want to hurt his feelings. Better just go along with it for the time being. And anyway, who cares? *I might as well be here as anywhere. And what was I intending to do anyway* when I got to Seyrac – scoop up a handful of gravel and chuck it at Jack's window? She squirms with the shame of it. For all she knows he isn't even there, he's somewhere in Aubrillac, or maybe Toulouse, shagging all night with someone else.

Damien's right about the lake, though. When they turn into the Truite d'Or car-park she catches her breath. The expanse of water is almost circular, flattened just slightly by the line of the dam over on the far side, fringed by a sandy beach – man-made, presumably. In the moonlight the surface reflects the dark hills without even a ripple. 'Do you see?' he says.

She nods. It's almost too much. It's been such a terrible day.

'If you like we can swim.'

'I haven't got a swimsuit.'

'You don't need it.' She hears the click as he releases his seat-belt. The next moment he's leaning across to kiss her, his lips soft and firm and practised, his tongue already trying to make her own mouth open in response. He tastes of wine and tobacco. In spite of herself she wants him to go on.

He's so different from Jack. She wants to cry suddenly. The kiss has made her body ache in a way it never really has with Jack or even with Jason, she can feel she's wet already. And yet she doesn't want to, she doesn't want this, she doesn't want anyone. She pulls away from him, shivering. 'I'm tired. Will you take me home?' Her mouth feels weird as she says it – she doesn't know where to put her tongue. Like when I was a kid, being kissed by some warty old aunt . . . He's disgusting. *And yet*.

He looks at her as if she's gone completely crazy. 'But there's no reason to be afraid. Let me show you.' His hand's inside her T-shirt now; she can feel his fingers moving up across her breast, catching and twisting at her nipple. A pulse swells and beats in the space between her legs. 'No.' His smell surrounds her – red wine and French aftershave and that sweet smell that means garlic but isn't like garlic at all. She hears her own voice, hoarse with something she can't even put a name to. 'No. Damien, stop it. Please. No!'

But it's too late. His hands are all over her, pulling at her trousers. She hears something rip. 'You want it, you know you do.' She feels him say it into her neck, his hands still groping, his breath all through her hair.

She wriggles away from him and pulls herself up into a sitting position. The door-handle jabs at her lower back. 'You kidnapped me. I was going to Seyrac. You made me come here with you.'

'And you didn't want to see this beautiful lake, of course not. When I started kissing you you didn't like it, you didn't feel something in your body, you said, "No, thank you Damien, you are very attractive but I am promised to another."' His mocking voice refuses to be silent, echoing in her ears, filling the stale metal box of the car. She can't listen. She fumbles behind her for the door-handle and half falls out, on her knees in the dirt. 'You fucking English bitch! You all think you can come here and buy everything with your filthy *pounds sterling!*' He sneers as he says it. 'You are the lord in his castle, you take our work, you make our houses expensive so if we want to stay here we can't buy them. And there is nothing here for us. Nothing! Our life is in the town now. And you come in after to eat up the dead farms and villages. You are vermin. Do you hear me? *Vous êtes dégueulasses.*' He kicks out at her and she falls over, her cheek scraping the gravel, something like a burn flaring at the side of her right knee. She pulls herself to her feet and goes to run.

But he's got her by the ankle. She tries to shake him off and almost falls again. He's lying half-in, half-out of the car, his face craning up at her from thigh-level, mouth hanging half open, cheeks lined with vertical creases. He's grinning. He's actually grinning. She twists to grab the car door with both hands and slams it as hard as she possibly can.

She feels the impact of the blow right through her body – a sharp pain in her right shoulder, a tendon in the back of her hand stinging like flicked elastic. The door swings back half-open and she has a momentary glimpse of the back of his neck, the place on the side of his head where the metal edge must have made contact. But at least he isn't coming after her any more. She bends down and rubs at her ankle. She can't close her fingers. Her whole body's starting to throb. There's blood running down the inside of her leg.

The moon's disappeared, but the clouds where it was are still backlit and silvery. She walks unsteadily down the beach towards the water, her feet sinking and turning in the soft sand. She reaches the edge and stoops to untie her trainers, struggling to undo the knots. It hurts. But the water, when she feels it on her bare skin, is cool. *He almost raped you. You're supposed to feel dirty.* But it isn't true. She feels clean, cleaner than the water. She takes another step forwards, immersing her hands. She's up to her hips, her chest, her shoulders. She turns and sees the car, parked where he left it, the two doors still wide open, and something dark in the gap, that could almost be shadow. He hasn't moved.

She's out of her depth now. She waits, treading water, watching to see how long it'll take him to struggle to his feet.

In a few minutes he'll stand and stretch and get back in and pull both the doors closed. He'll switch on the headlights. She'll hear the cough of the engine, the crunch of gravel under the tyres as his lights sweep the surface of the lake and turn uphill in a wide arc, then lose themselves in an occasional glitter between the trees.

The water's warm. She swims slowly out towards the centre. It's like leaving a con-trail across the night sky. For a long time, out at the centre of the lake, she hangs almost motionless, moving her arms and legs as little as she can get away with, turning in her small space to look at the broken reflections, the stars, the dark shapes of the hills. She's still alive, anyhow. After a while she tastes salt in her mouth. The tears are running down her face, mixing with the lake water. She ducks under the surface and comes up spluttering, pushing her hair back, feeling the air suddenly cold on her wet face. *There's only this — my body still managing not to sink, the water.* She turns over on her back and floats, opening her eyes wide to the emptiness, letting the universe flow in.

ACKNOWLEDGEMENTS

I'd like to express my warm thanks to the Virginia Center for the Creative Arts at its French outpost, le Moulin à Nef in Auvillar, Tarn-et-Garonne, for time and space to work intensively on this book, and to Jen and Chris Hamilton-Emery, as well as to Mara Bergman, Bridget Collins, David Constantine, Rachel Cusk, Clive Eastwood, Jerry Harp, Caroline Price, Frances Rae, Sarah Salway and Mary Szybist for their insights and/or support at different stages.